INVADERS OF THE HEARTLAND

James Bultema

P.D. Publishing

Also by James Bultema

Fiction

Sea of Red

Attack From Within

Red Lines

Non-Fiction

Guardians of Angels: A History of the Los Angeles Police Department 1869-2019

The Protectors: A Photographic History of Police Departments in the United States

Unsolved Cold-Case Homicides of Law Enforcement Officers

Gangsters and Cops: Prohibition, Corruption, and LAPD's Scandalous Coming of Age

Documentary

Behind the Badge: An Insider's History of the Los Angeles Police Department

Website: https://www.jamesbultema.com

P.D. Publishing – Scottsdale, Arizona

Edited by Karen Stoff, www.vocostoff.com, and Jennifer Duty, Jen4editing@yahoo.com

Cover design by Momir Borocki - Proi!

Author photograph by Carole Bultema

Dedication

To the small-town cops and sheriffs across this great
country.

Your unwavering commitment, quiet courage, and steadfast
dedication often go unnoticed but never unappreciated. You
are the heartbeat of the communities you protect, standing
guard when others sleep and holding the line when times
grow uncertain.

This book is dedicated to you: the guardians of the
forgotten roads, the peacekeepers in places where everyone
knows your name, and the heroes whose stories deserve to
be told.

SO FAR, EVERYTHING HAD gone according to plan—almost too well. "All F-units, F-10, suspect still northbound Van Nuys approaching Sherman Way," advised D-III Jake Dalton, the lead detective of the Los Angeles Police Department's Gang and Narcotics Division Fugitive Detail. "We're turning off. F-13, pick up the tail. F-12, parallel the route and keep out of sight."

"F-13, roger that."

"F-12, on that route now."

As Jake made a left turn to take them off the tail, his partner, D-II Rodney "Robbie" Robinson, pulled on his beard as he always did whenever he was thinking and talking at the same time. "We had him in front of us. We've got the warrant. We've got the units. I say take him down now."

"Look, Robbie," Jake glanced over at his partner of four years, "we know Rawlins has an associate in these bank robberies, but we still don't know who the fuck he is. Two men committed the last three bank robberies. We need to see if he leads us to dipshit number two."

"I hear ya, but we've got the big kahuna right in our sights. I would—"

"All F-units, F-12. Rawlins has pulled behind United California Bank at 21321 Van Nuys Boulevard."

Things were suddenly picking up. Jake could tell because the old burn scars on his arms started to itch, a sure sign of trouble ahead.

"All F-units, F-13. We have a suspicious vehicle, a newer gray Toyota Camry, just pulling up in front of the bank with two white males between twenty and twenty-five years old. Passenger is getting out, wearing a blue sweatshirt and jeans. He's rubbernecking the area. I think this is our second suspect."

"All F-units, F-12. Rawlins is checking the area and entering the bank's back door."

"All F-units, F-10. Set up diagonal deployment. Make sure we have all exits covered. For now, stay in your vehicles. F-10 has the northeast corner."

"F-14 has the southwest corner."

"Control, F-10."

"Go ahead, F-10."

"F-10 is Code 6 at UCB at 21321 Van Nuys Boulevard, on an investigation. We have four plainclothes units involved."

"All Van Nuys units, Control. F-10 reports he and three other units are Code 6 at UCB, 21321 Van Nuys Boulevard, on an investigation. No further details at this time."

Inside the branch of United California Bank, security guard Alexander Washington had only been assigned to UCB for two days—and he'd only been a guard for four days. He was there because he had just fulfilled the minimum requirements by completing eight hours of his forty-hour training, allowing him to be assigned a job. Now, with eight hours under his belt and a gun on his hip, he was patrolling the bank's interior. His boss—if you could call him that—had told Alex he was to monitor the bank's security cameras, patrol the interior and exterior, and maintain a visible presence to deter criminal activity.

Visible presence wasn't a problem for Alex. Carrying 350 pounds on a five-foot-eight-inch frame, Alex was a walking fire plug. As for his .45-caliber semiautomatic, he'd only learned how to put the magazine in and to chamber a round but had yet to fire it. He had no idea what double action meant or why his boss had mentioned the finger pressure needed to fire the first round, but he figured, Whatever. He was scheduled for sixteen more hours next week, including time at the range, which he was excited about.

As he shuffled along patrolling the bank's interior, Alex saw a man wearing a blue Dodgers cap enter through the back door. The man moved with urgency, his eyes darting around. Without warning, he yanked a large handgun from the back of his waistband. Alex's gaze locked with the stranger's—then came the gleam of metal as the barrel swung toward him. He had never stared down the business end of a gun before—not even his own. His body froze mid-step, his mind racing through the seconds that could decide his very existence.

"Don't even think about it, Mr. Security Officer," Rawlins said.

What went through Alex's head the moment he went for his weapon will never be known. He managed to clear it from his holster and bring it up, aiming it right at the man. He started to pull on the trigger and thought how strange it was that the trigger was so hard to pull back. He was so focused it didn't even register that Rawlins had shot his Smith & Wesson S&W500 at him or that a .500 magnum round had hit him in the forehead. His last vision was nothing but black as his head was blown apart, leaving his brain matter in a ten-foot radius around him.

"Control, F-10. Shots fired at our Code 6 location. Officer needs help, possible 211 in progress at UCB."

Immediately, Jake heard sirens in the distance.

"F-10 to F-12 and F-13. Deploy on foot. We have three suspects. One is in a getaway car out front, which we will handle. Two are in the bank. Do not let them outside our perimeter. F-14, stand by in your vehicle until black-and-whites arrive, keep them on the perimeter, and then join us."

As soon as Jake ended his transmission, he looked at Robbie. "You ready?"

"Roger that," he said.

"Split up and come up on the suspect from the rear."

"Got it," said Robbie. "Let's also keep an eye on the bank in case the dipshit comes looking for his ride."

"Agreed. Let's go."

After exiting their vehicle, both men threw on body armor and jackets with LAPD FUGITIVE DETAIL written on them to identify the plainclothes officers as the good guys. They drew their Kimber Custom II semiautomatics with chambered-in .45 ACPs and approached the gray Toyota Camry from extreme angles.

Jake saw that the suspect's window was down and noted he kept glancing at the bank's front door. As Jake drew down on the man in the car, he yelled, "Driver, police! Put your hands out the window. Do it now."

The suspect looked at Jake and then quickly glanced back at the bank.

Robbie had found cover while maintaining a bead on the driver.

Jake repeated his command, "Driver, put your hands out the window."

The suspect kept glancing back at the bank but did nothing else.

Shots rang out again from inside the bank. Suddenly, the Toyota took off. After going about forty feet, he was rammed on the driver's side by F-14. The impact sprayed glass in all directions but stopped the car in its tracks. Both detectives from F-14 exited their vehicle, deploying on the suspect just as Jake and Robbie came up from behind.

More shots echoed from inside the bank.

"Suspect down," yelled the driver from F-14.

"Put your hands where I can see them," his partner yelled at the suspect, but there was no movement.

Covered by the other detectives, the F-14 driver carefully opened the Toyota's door and dragged the bloody suspect out and onto the ground, then handcuffed him.

Jake saw the black-and-whites arriving. "Control, F-10. Have all patrol units form a perimeter to stop anyone from coming or going. Stay away from the bank. We have shots fired. Armed plainclothes detectives are in the area."

As Jake sprinted to the bank's front door, he heard Control repeating his information over the radio as he entered, holding his weapon out in front, finger alongside the frame. He immediately saw Blackwell from F-12, down and not moving, covered in blood. A few feet away, a civilian wearing a blue sweatshirt was down with a pistol a few inches from his hand. He was also bloody and not moving.

Blackwell's partner yelled, "Jake, Rawlins has a hostage and is ordering us to pull back."

As Jake worked his way through the bank, attempting to stay behind cover, he spotted Rawlins with his long-barreled gun pointed at the head of a thirty-something woman. She stared at Jake, her deep blue eyes wide but otherwise showing little emotion—no screaming, no crying, just staring at Jake.

Good for you, Jake thought.

"Listen, guys," Rawlins yelled while looking around, "I'm going to my car with my darling here. Lower your weapons. If you even so much as flinch, I'll kill her."

Jake took small steps to get a better shooting angle.

Rawlins snapped his head towards Jake. "Hey, hero, stop fucking around," he said. "Lower your gun, or it's all over for the missus here."

Since the asshole had seen him, Jake stopped and lowered his gun so it pointed at the floor. The hostage remained composed—just staring at him.

Jake was determined not to let Rawlins out the door with her, thereby losing all control of the situation and the hostage.

"Rawlins, come on, man, police are everywhere. They won't let you through. Give it up now, and I'll ensure it's reflected in my report."

Rawlins started shuffling backward toward the rear door, hiding behind the hostage. In another five feet, he would be outside.

Now resisting, the hostage began to jerk around in his grasp. Rawlins smacked her on the head with the barrel of his gun. "Don't do that, bitch, or I'll shoot you now."

Her reply was a deafening scream as she stomped on Rawlins's left foot with all her might, then attempted to collapse to the floor.

When Rawlins hit the woman, Jake's gut instinct told him to be ready for the woman to make a move. As she dropped down, he quickly brought up his gun and fired two rounds. Both shots struck Rawlins in the head, splattering the hostage with blood and brains as she crumpled to the floor without so much as a whimper.

Jake carefully approached Rawlins and, although he was clearly dead, handcuffed him and picked up his weapon. Robbie ran to the hostage, helped her to her feet, and got her behind cover.

"Control, F-10," said Jake. "Officer down, need paramedics. Three suspects in custody." As he moved toward Blackwell, the rest of the units entered. "Check out the suspect and secure the area," he ordered.

Bending over his friend who was on the floor, Jake saw blood coming from Blackwell's right shoulder and left leg. The detective's eyes opened slowly. "For Christ's sake, Jake, I don't need you. Get me somebody who knows what they're doing."

"Just what I thought. You needed a few extra days off, so you went and got yourself shot." Blackwell started to laugh but winced from the pain and quit talking.

One of the other Fugitive Detail detectives handcuffed the man across from Blackwell and yelled, "Jake, Suspect Two is dead."

While Jake acknowledged and relayed the info, Blackwell still didn't say anything. He was just happy to be alive.

Outside, black-and-whites covered the area as some brass started arriving. Jake knew it wouldn't be long before someone from the Force Investigation Division would show up, and then his detectives would be separated and interviewed late into the night.

"Jake," yelled Robbie, "over here."

"Coming." He squeezed Blackwell's good arm as he saw the paramedics quickly approaching, then went to Robbie.

After turning the corner at the teller cages, Jake stopped when he made eye contact with the same blue eyes he had stared into just a few minutes ago. It was the hostage. She was covered in blood but seemed not to care. Sitting in a chair, she stared up at him, looking as calm as she did when Rawlins threatened to splatter her brains all over the bank.

"Jake, this is Samantha Taylor. She wants to thank you."

It was hard to break the spell of her deep blue eyes. They were so intense that he had noticed them even during one of the most traumatic moments in both their lives.

She got up, came over, and offered her bloody hand to him, seemingly without a second thought. Jake took it gingerly, but she gave him a firm handshake.

"Sir, I really don't know how to say this, or if there are even words to express one's feelings when just a few minutes ago I thought I would be dead. When that man moved me backward to leave the bank, I knew it was probably the end for me."

Jake stared at the woman, wondering why he couldn't come up with anything to say.

"When I saw you come into view," she said, "I immediately felt a twinge of hope that I might actually survive."

That propelled Jake to speak. "I must say, Miss, you were the calmest hostage I've ever encountered. When we made eye contact, I could see in your eyes that we had a fighting chance and then some."

"Well, sir—"

"Please, call me Jake."

"Okay, Ja—"

"Jake, Higbee just showed up," Robbie said.

"Sorry, Miss—"

"Please call me Sam. All my friends do."

"Sure. Sam, I gotta go, but if you still want to discuss it, here's my card. Give me a call."

SEVERAL HOURS AFTER THE shooting, as Jake Dalton drove home in his lava-orange 2018 Porsche Cayman 718, he thought about the direction of the Force Investigation Division team's questioning. It seemed to him that they'd forgotten who the bank robbers were and who the good guys were.

Jake wondered how his dad, Earl, would have handled the FID's grilling. His dad was gone now, but Jake would never forget the wisdom of the hardworking auto mechanic who had run a small repair shop in Fairview, Oklahoma, a quaint town of 2,342. Earl had taught him to have a strong work ethic and a practical, hands-on approach to problem-solving. Jake remembered how much his dad had valued perseverance and integrity—and how that had rubbed off on him. Dad had always said that a man's worth was in the quality of his work and the strength of his word.

Jake chuckled as he thought of how his mom, Agnes, had balanced his dad's teachings by nurturing Jake's intellectual curiosity and ensuring his moral compass was correctly set. She had encouraged him to read widely and to think critically, always emphasizing the importance of empathy and justice.

Earl and Agnes had given him a strong character foundation, but tonight he'd been up against police bureaucrats who weren't like anyone or anything he'd ever encountered. Jake knew the lead detective of the FID team from his days in the elite Metropolitan Division. Lieutenant Mark Higbee was a big man. He had a reputation for helping officers when he saw them digging a hole they didn't want to fall into. For whatever reason, that hadn't been the case earlier during his interrogation, which was officially called a debrief.

"Detective Dalton," Higbee had said an hour after the shooting, "you stated that even your partner was encouraging you to take Rawlins off the street when it appeared the table was set for his arrest. Understanding he was an armed and dangerous bank robber with at least fourteen heists, why didn't you listen to your partner?"

"Come on, Higbee. You and I worked Metro for several years. We both know you want to get as much shit as possible on a suspect before the arrest. We also needed to get the accomplice, and if we took out Rawlins on Van Nuys Boulevard, then the accomplice would have been a free man who could commit who knows what crimes. Those guys were professionals, and we needed to get both."

"Well, how'd that work out? Never mind. At any point during your surveillance of Rawlins, did you think it was unsafe to arrest him?"

Jake looked at the big detective and, unblinking, answered, "No."

"When both suspects entered the bank, why didn't you send a team to monitor?"

"I decided it was safer to keep us out of the bank. A confrontation inside might have led to a firefight where innocent civilians could have been killed."

Higbee adjusted his massive hands on the table, folding them together. "But perhaps if you had deployed a team into the bank, they might have saved the security guard's life, don't you think?"

"Look, I'm sorry for any loss of lives, no matter who they were. And who's to say that the first shot we heard when we were in our vehicles wasn't the one that took out that security guard? I still believe my decision was correct. There could have easily been more bloodshed."

"What about you taking the shot at Rawlins when he had a hostage in his grasp and was using her as a shield?"

"In about five move steps, Rawlins would have been out the back door with the hostage, and then we would have lost all control. With inexperienced patrol officers on the perimeter, it could quickly have gone sideways for our hostage. The woman acted bravely to get out of Rawlins's hold, which allowed me to take two shots—I might add, two shots from me, a distinguished expert and a former SWAT sniper. I was confident that if I had a shot, I would succeed. I did, and saved the hostage's life."

Higbee looked down at his notes. "So, eventually, you sent in your units after hearing a gunshot, and one of your men went down. Why not set up your deployment and wait for the suspects to exit the bank rather than go blind into a situation that was already escalating?"

"Because that is exactly what you would have done, Higbee. I need a break."

Jake jumped up from his seat and went outside to get a breath of fresh air. Looking up into the city's luminous sky, he could hardly distinguish a single star. He thought how sad it was because back in Fairview, he would have seen a whiteout of shining stars.

Chapter 3 – The Cheng Syndicate

STANDING ON THE ROOFTOP of a decrepit building typical of the industrial area of Fuzhou in Fujian Province, China, Li Cheng peered through night vision binoculars at a well-lit warehouse across the street. Li couldn't help but be distracted by the low moon casting a silvery glow over the labyrinth of alleys and towering skyscrapers surrounding his target, the nerve center of his enemy, the Black Lotus Syndicate.

This was a life-altering day for the twenty-eight-year-old son of Ming Cheng, the Dragon Head of the Cheng Syndicate. Standing just shy of six feet and looking the part of a gangster, Li had jet-black hair combed straight back and sharp, almost-black eyes that seemed to see everything. As the eldest son and fifth-generation member of the family business, Li had been groomed for this day. It was time to demonstrate his ability to uphold and further the Syndicate's interests and earn its members' respect and trust.

The Black Lotus Syndicate, led by the ruthless Zhang Long, had been encroaching on Cheng territory by pushing drugs and weapons on their streets. This challenge couldn't go unanswered. Cheng Ming's orders were clear: Send a message that the Cheng Syndicate would not be messed with. Li's team of enforcers was eager to prove its worth.

"What do you have, Boss Li?" asked his most trusted lieutenant, Zhi Hao.

"Zhang Long is in there with at least six other fighters, all armed. They have one guard out front and another on the roof. Put Plan A into action." Zhi Hao repeated his boss's orders to the crew. Both men moved to ground level.

Li's best shooter was left behind on the roof, armed with a China North Industries Group QBU-88 suppressed sniper rifle, also known as the NORINCO Type 88. The former People's Liberation Army sniper put the crosshairs of his scope center mass on the guard on the roof, approximately 140 meters away.

A homeless man appeared on the sidewalk outside the Black Lotus Syndicate's warehouse. He wore several layers of dirty clothes, had a cigarette butt stuck between his lips, and half-walked, half-staggered to the guard at the entrance.

The door guard winced at the stench of the filthy man who smelled like he hadn't bathed in his entire life. "Get the fuck out of here," the guard ordered, and motioned with his arm for the man to move away. "Keep going."

"Please, I just need a light." The man shuffled closer.

"I'm warning you old man, keep moving or—"

The homeless man swiftly tossed aside a corner of his poncho, revealing a suppressed 9mm pistol. He fired one round. The door guard collapsed like a rag doll with a bullet through his right eye.

At that same instant, the sniper fired two rounds, the first striking the roof guard in the center of his chest and the second going through his head before he hit the ground, spraying brain matter all over the roof.

Li, armed with a China South Industries Group Type 5 submachine gun, plus a 9mm on his hip, led his entry team of six into the sprawling warehouse. Looking for any movement, they immediately spread out right and left. What they saw was a vast maze of metal shelving and towering stacks of crates, but no targets. The team split up and went down the long aisles.

Bringing up the rear, Zhi Hao and his five men found cover as they entered and then maintained those positions. Li's top lieutenant carried an assault rifle and a semiautomatic pistol.

The assassins moving down the aisles came to a crossroad of towering shelves, like the cliffs of Mount Husahan. Sneaking a peak to the right, Li was greeted with a barrage of gunfire. He laid out return fire toward the muzzle flashes coming from a second-story level. Bullets whizzed off the metal shelving, throwing hot sparks all over him and his men.

Li barked out, "Suppressing fire, now." His crew responded immediately with a barrage of bullets, which pinned down the Black Lotus shooters.

Crouching behind a stack of crates, Li assessed the situation. Using comms, he ordered, "Zhi, flank them on the left. Xiao, secure the high ground."

Zhi led his team through a narrow metal valley. Emerging on the left flank of the Black Lotus shooters, he caught them off guard. He and his men opened fire, their shots finding their targets with deadly accuracy.

With many of the enemy pinned down, Xiao and his two men climbed a stack of crates and secured a vantage point overlooking the Black Lotus position. From there, they provided cover fire and picked off those in the open.

Li and his team moved to gain a more strategic position. While moving to cover, he saw the leader of the Black Lotus Syndicate take off for a back room. Putting down his submachine gun, Li yelled for his men to cover him, then ran between stacks of crates as bullets ricocheted around him.

Working his way to a large office door, Li peeked in but saw no movement. Pulling out his 9mm, Li opened the door and dove to the floor. He felt a burning sensation on his right shoulder. He came up in a shooting position, scanning the room for Zhang. He spotted him between a large desk and a wall. Zhang didn't hesitate taking aim at Li, pulling the trigger on his assault rifle. Instead of the report of a round being fired, the firing pin landed on an empty chamber. The click echoed through the room.

Li ran the short distance to him with his 9mm aimed at Zhang Long's head. "Don't even think about it, or I'll plant a bullet right between your eyes."

Zhang Long, a natural-born killer at forty-one, dropped his assault rifle, but his right hand remained frozen as if his brain was calculating a response. Li helped him with his life-and-death decision and fired two rounds into his head. After Zhang Long collapsed, Li thought how interesting it was that a man who was the leader of the Black Lotus Syndicate a second ago was now just another corpse in the winner-take-all fight between two of the most powerful Chinese syndicates.

Sitting at the small desk in his Topanga Canyon apartment in Canoga Park, Jake contemplated the last few days. He detested politics, both the no-shit government politics and the small-time crap like a homeowners' association telling you to mow your lawn. People went on power trips at all levels, and they always sucked the little guy into their BS—case in point: the Force Investigation Division for the Los Angeles Police Department.

On paper, FID would gather all evidence and complete a detailed report regarding tactics, decision-making, policy compliance, and witness statements. They reported their findings directly to the Use of Force Review Board, which is comprised of deputy chiefs or above. They, in turn, made official recommendations to the chief of police with a final determination of whether the shooting was in or out of policy, whether tactics and judgment were appropriate, and whether further training or discipline was needed.

However, as with any oversight body, there could be perceptions or accusations of political motivations depending on the actions taken, the findings published, and the broader political context. Critics could always allege partisan bias.

Jake was a believer in that. Immediately following the shooting, the department notified him that he and his unit were being put on paid administrative leave. At the same time, the FID would conduct a full investigation into the events surrounding the shooting. Jake expected the investigation but disagreed with being taken out of the field. He told his friends that being put on administrative leave was pure bullshit. His was a good shooting, as was the entire operation—they had taken down three hard-core bank robbers. Jake had reason to believe politics played a part in the FID investigation because of a deputy chief who was on the board.

It happened five years ago when Jake was assigned to patrol: He arrested an eighteen-year-old for DUI after he caught him drag racing on a deserted side street lined with scores of kids partying and drinking. Jake quickly found out that the teenager was the son of then-LAPD Commander Richard Armstrong. During the booking process, the commander called Jake and said that he would be at the station in a few minutes to pick up his son—that there was no need to book him. When Jake told him that wasn't happening and explained the circumstances, all he got from the commander was, "Come on, Detective, we both know kids will be kids." When Jake again said no, Armstrong screamed something about getting even, and hung up. Five years later, that kid's father was a deputy chief on the review board.

Jake trusted the system and decided to let everything play out because he felt confident that what they were investigating wouldn't get anywhere, considering this new age of transparent policing.

What got him, though, was how some in the press had reported that three people were dead and that Jake was the reason. They alleged that if Jake and his detail had stopped Rawlins before he went into the bank when they had had the opportunity, those deaths at the bank could have been averted, and the hostage wouldn't have had to go through such trauma.

Now, because he had done his job, he sat in his apartment, staring at his computer. He was bored to death. Being on administrative leave sucked. He loved the streets and wanted back out there.

Outside of police work, he had little else going on besides being a Porsche Club of America chapter member. He enjoyed their monthly dinners, fun drives, and especially their High-Performance Driver Education program, which allowed him to put his Porsche through its paces on road courses.

He didn't date. Because his job had him working outlandish hours on different days each month, his schedule was too erratic to sustain a relationship. He figured he was a homebody, but so what? It worked for him. As he pondered his personal life, he saw an email from Anne of the Fugitive Detail come in.

> Hi Jake, I thought you might like to know, since I'm sure you're so busy, LOL, that the hostage from the bank shooting called for you and asked that you "please" give her a call. I hope all is well. We miss you around here. It's way too quiet! —Anne

Jake stared at the attached phone number, wondering why this woman would call. He sure as hell didn't know, but she deserved a call back for no other reason than that she probably saved both their lives when she screamed and stomped on the asshole's foot—which had been a great move and had worked almost as well as a flash-bang. He called her.

She answered on the first ring. "Hello, this is Sam."

He'd spoken to her once before, but it was like hearing her voice for the first time. He guessed it felt that way because this time no one was trying to kill them.

"Hi, Ms. Taylor. This is Detective Jake Dalton, LAPD, returning your call."

"My, don't we sound formal this afternoon? It's so much different from when I first met you, Detective."

Interesting, he thought. She had a dry sense of humor. He liked that. "What can I do for you, Ms. Taylor?"

"Please, Detective, it's Sam, remember? I feel you earned that right and then some."

Jake dropped his usual guard momentarily, and the words came out on their own. "Sure, Sam, and remember, I'm Jake."

"Okay, now we're getting somewhere. Jake, I reached out to you because two investigators came to my place asking questions about what happened at the bank. They said they were from the Force Investigation Division and were investigating the shooting."

Jake had expected that the FID would interview her since she was the principal witness to his actions and perhaps to the other shootings in the bank.

"Sure, I expected that, Ms. Tay—I mean, Sam. That's their job, and it's usually pretty straightforward."

"I get that, but I didn't expect some of their questions. Listen, I would feel more comfortable talking to you face-to-face. Would you have a problem with that?" She hesitated before adding, "Damn it, Jake. You saved my life, and it sounds like these jerks have motives other than getting at the truth."

Always fast on his feet, Jake quickly ran by where this was going. First, the LAPD was strict about turning an on-duty contact into a personal relationship, which this wasn't, but he wouldn't put it past the department to try and set him up. But since he was on administrative leave, he couldn't call her into the office to talk with her—

"Jake?"

"Sorry, you had me thinking. I'm on administrative leave, so we can't meet at my office. What did you have in mind?"

"You know Honeybee's House of Breakfast on Adams?"

"Sure do. I used to eat there years ago, back when I was working patrol."

"How about tomorrow morning at say, seven?"

"Sure, works for me, see you then."

"Thanks. I think this is important," she said before hanging up.

Chapter 5 – The Meeting

IN THE OFFICE OF a low-key industrial building in Fujian Province, they were all there, the heart and soul of the Cheng Syndicate. Ming Cheng sat at the head of a large ancient wooden table, peering through the thick haze of cigarette smoke. Sitting to his right was his son, Li, who felt more confident in his position in the syndicate after his defeat of Zhang Long and the Black Lotus gang. Sitting to the left of the Dragon Head was Zhi. Filling in the other eight chairs in the Syndicate's headquarters were the ranking lieutenants of the organization.

"Brothers," Ming Cheng began, his voice steady and authoritative, "we find ourselves at a pivotal moment in our operations. As you know, our traditional markets have become increasingly volatile and risky. Law enforcement agencies are tightening their grip, and our profit margins are shrinking due to escalating costs and competition."

Ming paused to allow his words to sink in. He noted that some of the senior men nodded in agreement, their expressions solemn. The Dragon Head continued, "The United States, primarily in a place called Oklahoma, presents us with a unique and lucrative opportunity. The legalization of marijuana in Oklahoma and twenty-eight other states has opened a gateway for an illegal distribution network, which we estimate could bring in forty billion dollars annually."

Ming got up and began to stroll around the table that had been the host of so many monumental decisions going back to 1907. "Oklahoma's marijuana industry is still in its infancy. There are regulatory loopholes and a relatively low level of scrutiny compared to the more established markets in California and Colorado. This makes Oklahoma an ideal location for us to set up operations. We can produce high-quality marijuana at a fraction of the cost and distribute it not only within the state but also to neighboring states where it remains illegal."

One of his senior lieutenants, a burly man with a scar running down his right cheek, leaned forward. "But why take such a risk? The US law enforcement agencies are formidable, and if we get caught, it could bring down the syndicate."

Ming stopped and then walked over to the senior lieutenant. "The risk is indeed high, but so are the rewards. The profit potential is immense, and by diversifying our operations into the US market, we reduce our dependence on traditional markets. The vast rural areas of Oklahoma provide us with the perfect cover to grow and distribute without attracting undue attention. I cannot stress enough that the rewards from this venture could be unprecedented."

Returning to the head of the table, Ming slowly took his seat. "Our strategy involves meticulous planning and execution. We will recruit local talent to avoid suspicion and establish a network of distribution channels that blend seamlessly with legitimate businesses. The key is discretion. We will leave no room for error in our operations."

Ming placed his hands on the table, leaning in slightly. "Remember, this is not just about money. It's about expanding our influence and securing our future. By establishing a foothold in the US, we send a message to our rivals and partners alike—we are adaptable, we are bold, and no border confines us."

Straightening up, Ming displayed a confident smile. "I have chosen my son, Li Cheng, to lead this operation. His recent triumph over Zhang Long proves his capability and loyalty. He also speaks excellent English. With him at the helm, I know we will succeed."

All around the room, there were murmurs of agreement and approval. Ming said, "Since my great-grandfather founded the Cheng Syndicate in 1907, we have grown and become more powerful with each generation. I see this venture as a continuum with my son, the fifth-generation leader, carrying the torch forward."

Chapter 6 – Hostage

If Jake had one fault, it was always showing up for an appointment early—very early. He couldn't explain why, but he usually arrived at least fifteen minutes earlier than the scheduled time. Hell, even when he played tennis with the boys, he got there thirty minutes early. He justified it by arguing he needed time to find the best no-ding parking space for his Porsche.

So here he sat in a corner booth at 6:45 a.m., waiting for the "hostage" to arrive at Honeybee's House of Breakfast. It was difficult for him to think of anything but the woman and how bravely she had dealt with the situation at UCB.

He was on his second cup of coffee when he saw her enter the restaurant—at 7:10. While such tardiness usually pissed him off, she came to the booth with such a big smile and warm greeting it made him forget all about the time.

"Hi, Jake. I'm so sorry. Traffic was a bear. I hope you weren't waiting long."

Unable to keep a smile from forming, he half-stood in the booth and pointed to the seat across from him. "No problem, Sam." He had remembered to call her that this time.

"You're so understanding. Good for you. I have friends who get so upset if I show up a minute or two late—but not you," she said with an even bigger, melt-your-heart smile.

The server, who had been eyeing the booth and waiting for Ms. Tardy, promptly came over, took their orders, and then left. Jake had noted Sam's dressy business attire. "Looks like you have an important appointment or do you always dress this nicely?"

Sam's face turned slightly red. "Why, thank you. I try to look the part when I must."

"What's the occasion?"

"Now that you mention it, I should explain. I'm fortunate to be the Curator of Anthropology at the Natural History Museum of Los Angeles County, and we're opening a new exhibit this afternoon. It's a new addition to our Dino World exhibit, and we have some VIPs coming in for a special showing."

"Wow, and here you sit, having breakfast with an LA cop. I'm honored."

Sam took a moment to gaze into Jake's eyes, "To say I'm still shaken by the horror at the bank would be an understatement. Try to imagine yourself as the hostage, and then a knight in shining armor enters your world by saving your life. It's a big deal, and I'm so thankful—I always will be." She reached over and squeezed Jake's hand.

Jake surprised himself by gently squeezing her hand in return. Almost immediately, they pulled back. He took a sip of coffee, and she fiddled with the collar of her blazer, both trying to downplay the brief contact that hinted at their pent-up emotions—feelings Jake rarely experienced or acknowledged. Fortunately, the arrival of Sam's orange juice spared them from discussing it.

As they chit-chatted through breakfast, Sam asked Jake about himself and his life before LAPD. He told her of his days growing up in Fairview and that he attended the University of Oklahoma after graduating from high school, earning a bachelor's degree in criminal justice.

It was odd how easy it was for him to continue his life story, how, at twenty-five, he moved to LA because of a desire for new challenges in a big city. So he joined the LAPD and quickly rose through the ranks, gaining a reputation for his sharp instincts and relentless determination. He explained that his colleagues often remarked on his ability to think several steps ahead, a skill he attributed to his father's methodical approach to repairing engines and his mother's emphasis on reading.

As they finished breakfast, Sam explained why she asked for this get-together. "Jake, as I told you on the phone, it seemed to me that the questions the two investigators were asking me about the shooting were slanted to elicit a response from me that would incriminate you."

Jake didn't like where this was going. "Can you be more specific?"

"They asked if I thought your actions in the bank were reckless and, in essence, endangered my life. They spent a lot of time on when you shot the man and if I felt like it was a bad move on your part. Almost every question they asked seemed to suggest that everything you did to save my life was reckless and irresponsible."

While she spoke, Jake shifted in his seat and could not keep eye contact with her. The old burn scars on his arms began to itch.

She paused momentarily and then said. "I'm not upset with you. I'm just worried about how these men seem to be after you, especially after you risked your life to save mine. I'm confused by it all."

Jake was pissed that the department would be coming after him for what most of his colleagues knew was a righteous shooting. Finally, looking into her blue eyes, he said, "Thanks for letting me know. I believe this has to do with a kid I arrested years ago for DUI, and now his father has influence over the men who questioned you. I have to believe that no matter how evil this man might have become, the system within LAPD will do the right thing."

Gently taking Jake's hand again with both of hers, Sam said, "I sure hope so. You shouldn't have to endure an investigation for actions that saved more lives than just mine."

He let her express her deep feelings instead of pulling his hand back again. But he also felt it was time to move on. "Thanks. Since you've got some important things happening today, I think I should let you get to them now."

After they both slid out of the booth, they found themselves standing close together. Jake felt a surge of emotions for this woman, feelings he couldn't quite define. It was all too new and bewildering for a bachelor who had spent his entire adult life alone. She gently hugged Jake, kissing him lightly on the cheek. Turning, she said, "Goodbye, Jake." And then she was out the door.

Chapter 7 – On the Move

AFTER HIS FATHER GAVE him the lead on his family's future, Li traveled on five flights over three days to Hong Kong to lessen the chances of a tail, paying close attention to those around him. He had his four carefully chosen operatives from the Cheng Syndicate do the same.

The syndicate members stayed separated as they checked into different rooms at the moderately priced hotel. They were in Hong Kong for one reason: to obtain the necessary forged credentials to enter the US without being caught. On the syndicate's payroll was a man known only as The Artist. He operated from a hidden workshop on a side street in a nondescript business area. The Artist had a reputation for creating documents so perfect they could fool even the most stringent immigration controls.

Arriving at The Artist's workshop at staggered times, each person marveled at all the high-tech equipment. Neatly aligned on the floor were various tools of the trade: high-resolution printers, embossing devices, ultraviolet light machines, and stacks of high-quality paper and plastic.

The Artist carefully printed each person's details onto passport pages, using a high-resolution printer that replicated the fonts and ink used by various government agencies. He then added photos that he had edited to blend seamlessly with the background.

Next, he turned his attention to the visas. He produced multiple entry visas for each, carefully matching the format and style of the US visa templates. He included details such as fake invitation letters, flight itineraries, and hotel reservations to support their cover stories. The visas were printed on high-quality paper with embedded security features. The Artist painstakingly added holograms and microprinting to make the visas appear genuine to even the most skilled agent.

For the driver's licenses, The Artist used specialized plastic cards that replicated US state-issued IDs, right down to the composition. He printed the operatives' cover names and photos onto the cards, adding barcodes and magnetic strips encoded with their information. To ensure authenticity, he used embossing techniques to apply the necessary state seals and holograms. He even integrated minor wear and tear on the IDs to make them look used.

After everyone got their new ID and supporting documents, Li split them up according to their unique cover stories. Li headed for Oklahoma City. The others traveled different routes, with some flying into Tulsa. All members of the Cheng Syndicate understood that everything came down to getting by US Customs and Border Protection.

After a flight that seemed never to end, Li stood in the immigration line at Will Rogers World Airport. Dressed in his new thousand-dollar business suit, Li told himself to look the part—be confident, be bold, and smile the entire time.

As he calmly walked up to the counter, he handed over his passport and visa with a look of respect for the American security officer. The middle-aged man scrutinized the Chinese citizen and then glanced at the documents.

"Business trip?" said the officer in a voice that indicated he asked the same question at least a thousand times each day. But while the agent acted casually, he knew what type of answer to expect and how to read the eyes of the person giving the reply. Everything he did and said came from his eighty-nine days of initial training and fourteen additional weeks under the watchful eye of a supervisor during a field training program.

Li was ready. "Yes, I'm attending a tech conference here in Oklahoma City." Li smoothly produced a forged invitation letter, which the officer waved off.

The agent gave him another once-over, looking for any hint of anxiety. Not seeing any, he looked down at the passport, stamped it, and handed it back to Li, "Welcome to the United States, sir."

While collecting his forged documents, Li smiled and said, "Thank you, sir." After getting his luggage, he turned to the exit sign and walked into the United States of America, ready to make billions for the family.

Chapter 8 – The Hearing

Six months after the shooting at UCB, the Use of Force Review Board had completed its investigation and called for a hearing to present its findings to the LAPD's chief of police. The chief would decide whether discipline was warranted and then present his decision to the Board of Police Commissioners. Today was that day. The review board's written report was comprehensive, detailing the events with a focus on the actions of the lead Detective III, Jake Dalton.

As the chief scanned those present in his conference room, he saw his good friend, Deputy Chief Richard Armstrong. Armstrong was a top-notch man with a good chance of replacing him when the chief retired. Whatever the findings, the chief was confident they would follow policy with no exceptions.

The room was neatly divided. The review board personnel filled one side of the long table. Jake, with his legal representation provided by the Police Protective League, was on the other. Jake glanced at Armstrong, who would be leading the presentation.

"Welcome, everyone," said the police chief. "We're all busy, so let's start this hearing, Deputy Chief Armstrong."

Armstrong stood. "Good morning, Chief. Thank you for meeting with us today. We've completed our investigation regarding the recent misconduct allegations involving Detective III Jake Dalton, the officer in charge on the day of the shooting. Today, I want to provide a detailed overview of our findings and offer recommendations to address the identified issues." Armstrong picked up a folder and read from it.

"We conducted interviews with witnesses, reviewed video footage, and analyzed relevant documents and policies. Our investigation revealed three findings. For Finding 1, D-III Dalton failed to take Rawlins into custody when the opportunity presented. Dalton had the officers, and the strategic advantage of taking the suspect into custody safely. By him not doing so, three people are dead, two were injured, and one is traumatized from being held hostage."

Jake was ready to yell bullshit, but his counsel sensed it, patted him on the elbow, and whispered, "Not now."

"For Finding 2," Armstrong continued, "D-III Dalton used poor judgment by ordering Frank-14 to ram Suspect 3's car. This tactic is not within LAPD policy when a vehicle is not equipped for such a maneuver. The order was reckless and dangerous."

Under the table, Jake curled his fingers into a fist.

"For Finding 3, D-III Dalton showed flawed judgment, ordering detectives to enter the bank when they had no intelligence on what was occurring inside the building. Department policy states that in this situation, they should set up exterior deployment and call for specialists, including the Hostage Rescue Team and SWAT. By rushing the interior of the bank without said intelligence, one officer was shot and two suspects were killed. Our investigators also noted that if the hostage had not acted for her self-preservation, she could have easily been another victim."

As Armstrong spoke, Jake could barely refrain from blurting out how this was all a sham, but instead, he forced himself to keep his mouth shut.

"As you know, Chief," Armstrong said, closing the folder, "the department must review all reports, consider all the evidence, and determine whether discipline is warranted. We are available for further consultation as needed."

"Thank you, Chief Armstrong." The chief looked over to Jake and his attorney. "Is there anything you want to add?"

"Yes, Chief," said Jake's attorney. "I would like to make a statement and then have Detective Dalton answer the allegations in his own words. Is that permissible, Chief?"

"Most certainly, Counsel. Please continue."

"Thank you, Chief. Just for the record, I want to give a brief background on Detective Dalton's exemplary career. Jake joined the LAPD ten years ago and was elected class president by his peers while in the academy. Not long after graduation, he received LAPD's highest honor, the Medal of Valor, when he rescued a mother and her ten-month-old baby from their burning SUV. Jake received third-degree burns on both his arms from this heroic rescue."

As if on cue, the minute the lawyer mentioned the medal, the scars on Jake's arms tingled. Jake ignored it, as always, and concentrated on what his attorney was saying.

"Jake was a sniper on the SWAT team, and then chose to be promoted through the detective ranks, where his numbers were always at the top of his division. Jake continues to excel as the youngest lead officer in the Fugitive Detail. As an attorney representing officers of the LAPD, I must say he is the most unlikely officer to be accused of inefficiencies I have ever encountered in my fifteen years of entering this building. But let me call on Detective Dalton to speak for himself about the questionable charges brought against him." Turning to Jake, he said, "Detective Dalton."

Jake looked around the room, glancing at everyone but letting his gaze stop for a moment on Armstrong. "Thank you. I appreciate the opportunity to address the allegations.

I take these charges seriously and want to provide a comprehensive account of my actions and thought processes." Armstrong looked away, perhaps knowing what was coming next. "But I want to go on record regarding an incident that occurred five years ago, as I feel it has a bearing on my case. Working patrol at the time, I arrested an eighteen-year-old for drag racing and DUI. During the booking process, I received a call from then-Commander Armstrong telling me that my arrestee was his son, and that he would be right down to pick him up as there was no need to book him. When I said no, he got belligerent, said something about getting even, and hung up."

Looking at the police chief, Jake continued, "The fact that Armstrong said he would get even makes me question his impartiality and the bearing it has on my case. I did my job then, and I did my job properly at UCB—"

"I object to these accusations," interrupted Armstrong. He sat back in his chair and looked at the chief, completely avoiding Jake's gaze. "What happened years ago has nothing to do with today's proceedings about a detective who made several wrong choices. He's falling back on innuendo to escape answering the charges."

The chief of police held up his hand. "Gentlemen, let's remain professional and stick to today's hearing. Chief Armstrong, please let the detective finish."

Jake said. "I don't believe we should second-guess decisions made in the seconds when volatile circumstances evolve. At the time of the incident, I assessed the situation based on the details as I knew them at that moment. My primary concern was the safety of all parties involved, including bystanders and fellow officers. At the time of the surveillance on Rawlins, we knew he was a career felon who had been arrested numerous times for armed robberies. I decided to follow Rawlins, hoping to locate the suspect who had been an accomplice in the previous two bank robberies. Taking Rawlins off the street early in our tail would have gained us nothing in identifying Suspect 2.

"Regarding Finding 2 concerning the ramming of the getaway car, I did not order this tactic. F-14 decided on his own to prevent the suspect from getting away."

Jake took a breath as he collected his thoughts. "Regarding Finding 3, the decision to enter the bank immediately rather than to wait for specialized units—sir, it was a fast-moving, developing robbery. I had the black-and-white units remain on the perimeter after we heard the first gunshot come from the bank. I decided that time was of the essence for the safety of all those involved. I ordered a tactical entry into the bank to neutralize the threat. We had the element of surprise on our side, and I decided to stop the robbery before it went any further. I believe that we saved the lives of innocent bystanders and bank employees by our actions. Unfortunately, as Detective Blackwell entered the bank, Suspect 2 saw him and fired, striking Blackwell twice. Blackwell, although wounded, returned fire and killed the suspect."

"As I entered the bank and moved toward cover, I encountered Rawlins holding a gun to the head of a woman. Rawlins was attempting to exit the bank with the hostage, which I knew I had to stop if given the opportunity. The hostage had remained calm the entire time, and I anticipated that she might try to escape or—as she did—create a diversion. When she screamed, stomped on Rawlins's foot, and dropped down, I was ready. I had a clear line of fire at the suspect and took it. You have the testimony from Ms. Taylor confirming what I just said. Also, she has since contacted me to thank me for everything I did to save her life. She said she would happily come here and testify on my behalf if needed."

The room was quiet as Jake paused. Armstrong gave Jake no notice and looked straight ahead. Jake continued, "I understand the seriousness of these allegations and the importance of maintaining public trust. I am committed to upholding the highest standards of conduct of the LAPD, and I believe I have done so. I wouldn't change a thing because I saved lives that day, and I respectfully request that you and the board consider my testimony and the evidence provided when making a decision. Thank you."

The room was silent for a few seconds, and Armstrong's adjutant said, "Thank you, Detective Dalton. We will carefully review your statement and the additional evidence provided."

The chief stood up and said, "If there's nothing else, this hearing is concluded. Thank you all."

Chapter 9 – Invaders

LI CHENG FELT INVIGORATED. He had cleared the US immigration checkpoint with hardly a bead of sweat. After exiting the airport, he headed for the shuttle that would take him to the car rental agencies. Once there, he used his forged driver's license and passport to rent a black Jeep Grand Cherokee.

His plan remained simple. His four operatives had flown into Tulsa and Oklahoma City at varying times. Li's second-in-command, Zhi Hao, who would closely supervise the operation, had gone to Tulsa, where he would rent a gray Chevrolet Traverse LT. Those not renting cars used various means of transportation to gather at the Super 8 Motel on the outskirts of Oklahoma City.

By 9:00 p.m., everyone had arrived at room 212. The three who joined Li and Zhi were Bin Wang, who would lead the business aspects of the operation. Mei Zhao, who would handle day-to-day operations, and Jun Zhou, in charge of distribution.

A travel map of Oklahoma was spread out over the queen-size bed, and the brain trust for planning the illegal marijuana grow center crowded around the bed. Li got the strategy session going.

"One of the keys to our operation will be identifying a discreet place with a low police presence where we can operate our extensive grow process."

"Boss Li," said the business manager and ex-military man, Bin Wang, "I had a two-man advance team reconnoiter the areas we thought looked promising in our pre-departure meetings. From their observations and research, I believe Fairview"—he pointed to a spot north of Oklahoma City—"is the town that should meet all our needs. The population is around twenty-four hundred, and their police department has five officers, including the police chief. My team learned that the mayor is having financial difficulties, so we may have some leverage there. I can work on getting leads on which property owners in the area are in serious debt, so any land sales won't seem suspicious. We should have both our frontman and property soon."

"Thank you, Bin," said Li. "Another critical area for us to concentrate on is getting the Chinese labor across the US-Mexico border and into Oklahoma. Zhi, I want you to ensure this happens quickly." Zhi acknowledged the order with a quick nod of his head.

"Jun, follow up on the list of legal growers in the state and provide us with a detailed report on all aspects of their operations." Jun nodded his head.

Looking over at the only woman involved in the operation, Li said, "Mei, integrate yourself into the local community quickly. Join the Rotary Club, attend town meetings, sponsor some local events, and most importantly, build relationships with key figures such as the chief of police, the mayor, and the members of the city council. I want our operation to appear to be a boost to the community."

"Yes, Boss Li," she said, slightly bowing her head.

"It's time to get to work," Li took the map off the bed. "You all have your own motel to stay in until we get our permanent location. Leave here in fifteen-minute intervals, and I'll be in touch to learn of your progress."

Chapter 10 – The Realtor

"You understand, sir, that this house has no water, electricity, or indoor plumbing, right?" said George Sullivan of Sullivan Realty in Fairview.

"Of course I do," said his client. "I don't need those things. Like I told you, I'm a businessman from Oklahoma City who has a hankering for self-sufficiency and independence. When the shit hits the fan, my friend, you're gonna wish you knew how to survive when the grid is no longer functioning."

As his client wandered around the property, George inwardly shook his head again at how he ended up selling houses that gave his profession a bad name. Not long ago, he'd sold properties in his hometown worth millions, making with one commission what most people made in a year. It was all good until he got run out of town for screwing the mayor's wife. After that romp, no one would even talk to him unless it was at the bar, and then it was only regulars who wanted to know if the mayor's wife was a good lay. He needed to keep a low profile for a while, and peddling shacks in Fairview was just the thing.

So here he was in Podunk, USA, trying to sell a house priced at $55,000. With that commission, he could make his mortgage payment, go to Rosie's, order a steak, and hopefully have enough money left for the tip.

Mr. Live Off the Grid walked up to him with the most enormous shit-eating grin he'd seen in a while. "George, let's write this baby up." George could taste that steak already.

That night at Rosie's, George was sitting alone in a corner booth and enjoying a steak that was so large it took over his plate. In between bites, something unusual happened. He saw an Asian woman enter and case the restaurant, seemingly looking for something or someone. It was strange because there was only one Asian family in the entire town, and she wasn't one of them. He knew—he'd sold them a house. They were Vietnamese and had opened a dry-cleaning business.

As he took another bite, he checked her out using his ten-point rating system. He always rated women. She appeared to be in her mid-thirties, like him, and had nice tits for an Asian. She had long, silky black hair that seemed to frame her tiny features. With a great figure in tight-fitting jeans, she moved closer to him, and he noticed pretty, almond-shaped, deep brown eyes. But before he could finish grading her, she walked straight over to him.

Shit, he thought, was she looking for him?

"Excuse me, Mr. Sullivan." She extended a tiny but impeccable-looking hand. "I'm Mei Zhao."

George almost choked as he swallowed his last bite. Meeting a hottie wasn't what he'd expected when he sat down for dinner. Being a man who always finished what he started, he mentally finished grading her and gave Mei a nine. She could have been a ten, but she was, after all, Asian.

"Well, hello," George said, ignoring her hand. "I must say, this is unexpected. How may I help you?"

She sat opposite him in the booth, ignoring his power play. "I am so sorry to bother you," she said, "but I have been trying to reach you for the last couple of days."

He knew that was a lie since he spent most of his time waiting for the phone to ring. "Well, I'm truly sorry about that. I've been busy with new clients and sales."

"I completely understand. I have heard that you are the man to see if one needs anything related to real estate in Fairview."

"Why, thank you. That's nice, and, by the way, true," he said.

"What I have to say is quite important and, as you will see, very lucrative for you if you are interested."

His attention doubled. "Please continue," he said with the warmest smile he could manage.

"Thank you," she said with a smile that outperformed his. "I represent Green Horizon Cultivation LLC, a company that wants to establish a marijuana-grow business here in Fairview. We require twenty acres for our commercial greenhouse operation and prefer something with a larger home on it. The property must have electricity and plenty of water available. And we are ready to proceed immediately. Would you be able to help us?"

George hesitated momentarily, as nothing but dollar signs flashed in his mind with *cha-ching* sound effects. Settling down quickly, he said, "Why, Ms. Zhao, you have indeed found the right realtor to get this done promptly. I will get on this tonight."

"One other thing, Mr. Sullivan. We would like you to be one of our investors. Don't worry—you don't have to put up any money. In fact, we would be willing to pay you handsomely for your services." She hesitated as George's eyes seemed to be twitching back and forth. "We would like you to put everything in your name—the deeds, the utilities, and that sort of thing—because my company likes to operate in the background."

Although excited, George replied calmly, "I see. I'll have to give this some thought. What kind of payment are we talking about?"

"How about $25,000 a month to begin with? We can adjust that when we see how things are working out."

George almost jumped out of his seat. To get $25,000 a month by just putting his name on the dotted line—he wanted to scream, Count me in. But what came out was, "Thank you, Ms. Zhao. I'm sure we can work something out. How about meeting with me in my office tomorrow at 1:00 p.m.?"

Standing, Mei thanked him and left through the door she had entered on a mission to change George Sullivan's life forever.

Chapter 11 – The Farmer

AS DAWN BROKE OVER the lush rice paddies of China's Hubei Province, Yong Chen was waking up. His first thought for the day was that no matter your age, transplanting season was the toughest time of the year. He glanced around the modest wooden house he shared with his family. His wife was preparing breakfast. The smell of congee and pickled vegetables drifted through the house, providing a brief but comforting distraction from his thoughts of the work ahead.

After a quick meal, Yong donned his wide-brimmed hat and stepped into his worn sandals. He felt the familiar squish of mud as he walked toward the fields. The morning mist hovered over the waterlogged paddies, creating an eerie, almost hypnotizing scene. But for Yong, this was no fairy tale. It was his daily routine, one filled with grueling work. With a bundle of seedlings in hand, Yong waded into a paddy, the water enveloping his legs. He bent over, almost folding in half, and began the backbreaking planting of each seedling into the muddy field.

Sweat dripped from Yong's brow. He paused occasionally to stretch his aching back and wipe his forehead with the back of his hand, leaving streaks of dirt

After ten hours of work in the paddy, he rested by a fire with several other villagers. They were discussing new opportunities in America. Two of the men talked of plentiful jobs and wages that were more than he could ever have imagined, especially in a place called Fairview, Oklahoma. Yong walked home in his muddy sandals, asking himself if America might be possible.

He shared his thoughts that night with his wife, who initially disagreed with his proposal. However, she saw the hope in her husband's eyes and agreed it was worth pursuing.

Determined to make his dream a reality, Yong sold their small plot of land, borrowed money from relatives, and collected his savings. A week later, he kissed his wife goodbye, promising to send money to her at her sister's, where she was staying.

Yong's journey began with a long train ride to Guangzhou. The trip was grueling. With scarce room on the rail car, he managed to squeeze in but had little food and water. He kept telling himself to stay positive. The smell of so many bodies crammed beside each other was disheartening, but it was a small price for the promise ahead.

He met a man in Guangzhou who specialized in arranging illegal crossings into the United States. The plan was risky, involving a flight to Mexico City and a treacherous journey to the US-Mexico border. When Yong arrived in Mexico City, he joined a group of migrants led by a coyote named Manuel. For a hefty fee, Manuel said he would guide them through the desert to the American state of Texas. He assured the group that he had made the trek many times and was skilled at avoiding detection.

On their first night, each person was allowed to carry only a tiny backpack with water, food, and a few personal belongings. They had to toss everything else. As the only Chinese man in the group of ten other migrants, Yong didn't talk much because they all spoke a different language. As they started their journey, Manuel explained their strategy to avoid detection by the border patrol, and, for the most part, Yong understood the basics because Manuel used his hands to convey his message. Yong and the others were to stay close, stay quiet, and follow Manuel's lead. They would travel at night and rest during the day. And they were to keep an eye on each other and not stray from the group.

Manuel avoided roads and well-traveled paths and used natural cover to stay out of sight. On the third night, Manuel suddenly raised his hand as they crossed an exposed, wide-open stretch of desert. Everyone stopped and remained silent. The noise of an engine preceded the sight of headlights cutting through the darkness. A vehicle was coming in their direction.

The group dropped to the ground and crawled toward a slight depression in the sand. They huddled together, subconsciously holding their breath as the vehicle approached. The headlights swept across the desert, illuminating the area around them. Yong's heart raced as the light passed over them, and he hoped they would remain unseen.

They listened silently as the vehicle stopped only feet from their hiding spot. Yong peeked and saw *Instituto Nacional de Migración* written on the vehicle door. The border patrol agents talked as they scanned the area with flashlights and bright spotlights mounted on the truck. One agent stepped out of the vehicle, his boots crunching on the desert floor. The man's flashlight illuminated the area around them as the footsteps grew louder. The man stopped, and Yong thought for sure he saw them. Then, the officer unzipped his pants and urinated no more than fifteen feet away from them. Suddenly, a loud noise like a gunshot echoed through the night. The man quickly zipped up his pants and ran back to the truck. It roared away a moment later.

Manuel held his hand up, signaling everyone not to move. After the engine noise faded, he whispered something and made a different signal. The group got up and went on their way a bit faster than before.

The following nights were a blur of cautious movement and tense moments. They navigated through the desert, crossed rivers, and skirted around small towns, constantly wary of patrols and checkpoints. Finally, after nearly a week of travel, they reached the border fence. Manuel guided them to a section of the fence where a small hole had been cut. Yong couldn't believe he was sneaking into America.

On the other side of the fence, the group was met by yet another coyote, and the migrants were taken to a safe house on the Texas-Mexico border. They had made it, and a day later, Yong set out on his own to find a way to Fairview, Oklahoma.

Chapter 12 – Enough Is Enough

As Jake entered the chief of police's conference room, he felt he was one man against the establishment. He first saw Armstrong, who was glaring at him and sitting at the table to the chief's right, the traditional position of honor. Also present were the captain of the training division, and assorted onlookers. Jake had been ordered to show up to receive the chief's decision about the UCB investigation.

Although Jake didn't wear a uniform while on duty, like every officer in the LAPD, he had one ready to go for an assortment of reasons. To him, this meeting was one of those reasons. His muscular six-foot frame filled the dark blue uniform, which had his Detective III rank neatly presented on a sleeve. His Medal of Valor hung near his left pocket, and just above that was his badge, polished to perfection. Two hash marks on his left lower sleeve indicated he had served in the LAPD for ten years or more, and a man could have shaved in the reflection of Jake's spit-shined boots. He looked sharp.

As he took his seat, the official LAPD Use of Force Incident Report was laid before him. He didn't touch it.

The chief opened the meeting by saying, "I want to thank all of you present for today's discussion of the Use of

Force Incident Report's key findings, analysis, and recommendations. The report's principal conclusion, which I agree with, deals with the initial surveillance of suspect Rawlins." The chief directed his attention towards Jake but didn't make eye contact. "Detective Dalton, none of this would have occurred, and we would not be meeting today, if you had ordered the stop and detention of Rawlins when you had the opportunity on Van Nuys Boulevard. Your decision to escalate the situation by letting Rawlins continue so you might identify a second suspect was not within department policies and procedures. Your partner questioned your decision not to stop Rawlins that day. I ask the same question today."

Jake felt every set of eyes in the room divert from the chief to him. He didn't move a muscle. Let the second-guessing continue, he thought, because his turn would come.

"When you followed Rawlins," the chief continued, "as so often happens, the tail escalated into a crime, this time a bank robbery. While your initial deployment on the UCB was sound, after hearing a gunshot, your decision to send your men into the bank without any internal intelligence or additional backup was not in keeping with the LAPD's policy regarding a robbery in progress. You should have maintained your exterior deployment while calling for the necessary units, such as the Hostage Rescue Team, SWAT, and other department resources."

The chief took a breath. Jake looked over at Armstrong and got a smirk in return. The prick was loving this.

Still not making eye contact with Jake, the chief went on, "Your decision to send your officers inside the bank during a robbery in progress resulted in an additional shooting, and the serious wounding of Detective Blackwell. This led to your encounter with Rawlins, which involved a hostage situation that could have, at any moment, turned deadly for the hostage."

The chief ruffled through his papers, picked up a single sheet, and began reading, "It is my conclusion that your decision not to take Rawlins into custody when the opportunity was present escalated events into a bank robbery, the death of three people, and the wounding of two others. Based on the investigations from our department, I therefore suspend you for thirty days without pay. You will turn in your badge and sidearm and will refrain from contact with the department during this period."

The chief set the piece of paper on the table but kept reading from it. "At the conclusion of the suspension, I order you to report to the training division for a week of remedial training on tactics and what is required by the policies of this department. After this training, you will report to your position on the Fugitive Detail. You may now address these findings to those present."

Jake took it all in—the moment, the look on Armstrong's face, the suspension—and made a decision that came from deep within his soul. He stood and looked into the eyes of the leader of the LAPD.

"Chief, with all due respect, this baseless decision is a slap in the face to my years of dedicated service to the citizens of LA. I have served this department with distinction for over ten years, earned commendations, and risked my life countless times for the safety of our city. To suspend me for a month and then mandate training is a gross overreaction.

"I've been in situations far more volatile than the UCB incident and have always acted in the best interest of public safety. My decisions before and during the bank robbery aligned with the department's protocols and my extensive training. To be told that my actions warrant such severe punishment is setting a bad precedent and jeopardizing the effectiveness of other officers on the force."

Jake took a second to contemplate his next move. He looked at Armstrong, who leaned back in his chair with his arms crossed over his chest. "I believe Deputy Chief Armstrong has held a grudge against me ever since I arrested his son." Jake turned his attention to the chief. "I also believe his influence had a bearing on your decisions. I've always loved and respected the LAPD and its leadership, but this political BS has proven that my respect was misplaced. Therefore, I resign from my position as a Los Angeles police officer, effective this minute."

Jake removed his badge from his uniform and his sidearm from its holster, carefully setting them down on the table. After making an about-face, he left the room without hesitation, even as the chief called for him to return.

Chapter 13 – Let's Call This Home

BY THE END OF THE meeting at his office, George Sullivan, the only broker and realtor at Sullivan Realty, knew precisely what was needed to please his client.

Fortunately, he had just listed such a property. Not only was there enough acreage, but there was a large three-story Victorian home that was up to code. The property was easily accessible yet remote enough to keep her company's operation under the radar. He and Mei drove out to view it.

When they turned down the unmarked access road, Mei immediately liked that aspect. "George, how many roads are there to the house and the surrounding twenty-three acres?"

George was happy he had done his homework when listing this property. "This unmarked entry road is the primary way in and out. There's one other dirt road a little to the north, but you could easily block that off. The previous owner couldn't get around very well for the past ten years, so he didn't upgrade the property's roads. But as you will see, he kept the house in top condition."

After going three-quarters of a mile, they pulled around a bend in the road and there it was—a massive Victorian home built in 1884. Having been born and raised in China, Mei wasn't used to such an enormous structure for just one family. Offset from the house was a large, sturdy barn neatly adorned in red with not even a chip of paint missing. She had plans for the barn right away.

As George showed her the home, barn, and surrounding property, Mei knew this was exactly what they needed. "What is the asking price?"

"First, I was able to negotiate a fair price with the one surviving relative who just wants the money and to be done with everything. We came up with $997,000 for the acreage and the home." George eyed Mei, trying to read her thoughts about the price. She was tight-mouthed for too long to suit him.

"No worries," he said. "I'm sure if I tell her I have an interested buyer so soon, I can get her to take less. What do you have in mind?"

"That won't be necessary," Mei said. "I have been looking for some time, and I feel that is a very fair price. Please write it up for an even million and offer it immediately. My associates are very anxious to get going with our new business."

Every time George was around Mei, he kept seeing dollar signs that seemed to get bigger with each encounter. "Of course, Ms. Zhao. Let's head back to town, and I'll write it up for one million."

"Thank you, and please, call me Mei. As a reminder, the home will be in your name. I will have a contract drawn up for you to sign indicating that we fronted the money. Does this work for you?"

Without hesitation, he said, "Yes, Ms. Zhao—I mean, Mei. Thank you."

"By the way, this will be a cash offer."

George just smiled.

Chapter 14 – Homecoming

HAVING SURVIVED THE DANGERS of his harrowing trip from China to the US, Yong Chen was now in a land where he understood absolutely nothing. He didn't comprehend the language, signs, culture, or vastness. At a rest stop in Texas, with just a few dollars in his pocket, he was looking at a map and trying to find Fairview, Oklahoma. While he was standing there in his tattered clothes, a large bus pulled up and released its passengers for a break. For nearly the first time since he left China, he saw words he could understand on the side of the bus belonging to a Chinese tour company.

As the people from the bus filtered past him, he asked several of them for help while pointing to the map. Most of the Chinese tourists barely acknowledged him and went about their business. Finally, an elderly woman approached him and asked what was wrong. He was so grateful that someone was talking to him in his native tongue that he started to weep.

"My son, what is the problem? I will help you," said the old lady. Heavy wrinkles creased her face but did not diminish her pleasant smile, which warmed Yong's heart.

He gathered his wits and told her he was looking for work in Fairview, Oklahoma. He showed her the map. While searching for it, both saw places they had never heard of.

Seeing the two staring at a map, a retired American professor of Chinese studies overheard their conversation and introduced himself. Yong and the woman looked at each other in clear disbelief that an American spoke their language. Yong told him what they were looking for. The man showed them where they were on the map and where Fairview was. He then went even further, pulling out his pocket notebook and quickly writing some words down in English:

Please Help Me

Going to Fairview, Oklahoma

NEED A RIDE PLEASE

The man showed Yong the note, told him what it said, and showed him the route. He suggested that Yong ask a truck driver for a ride. With that, he was gone. The old lady hugged Yong and slipped him twenty dollars, then returned to her bus and waved to him from the window.

All day, Yong walked among the big rigs, showing the professor's note to anyone who would take the time to look. Finally, he happened upon a truck driver from Taiwan who was now a US citizen. The man told Yong he could get him to Oklahoma City, but no farther. Yong expressed his gratitude and climbed into the passenger's seat. Coming from a small farmer's community in China, he couldn't believe the enormity of the truck. Four hours later, the driver dropped Yong off at a large truck stop in Oklahoma City and then went east.

After a few hours looking for a ride from other big rigs, Yong walked to the other side of the truck stop where the cars and pickup trucks were getting gas. It was tough getting anyone to even look at him. He guessed they thought he was going to ask for money.

More hours passed while he walked among the thirty or so pumps, but finally, he spotted a Chinese man putting gas in a black Mercedes SUV. As Yong approached, the man stared at him and initiated a conversation.

"Hi, may I help you? You look lost."

Yong, grateful to hear his native language again, replied, "Thank you, sir. I am looking for work and heard there might be some in Fairview at a marijuana grow."

Zhi Hao couldn't believe it. The man was obviously from China, looking to work for the Cheng Syndicate's grow operation. Zhi was immediately interested in the poor man, who was undoubtedly a farmer. "Well, this is your lucky day, as I am the man who does the hiring for our business in Fairview. Come closer."

Yong didn't hesitate and did as he was told. Zhi added, "Now turn around."

Yong did. Zhi had lived as long as he had in the underworld because he trusted no one, especially a ragged man who could be setting him up for an assassination. After all, his men had used the same ploy in China when they attacked a rival gang.

He searched Yong thoroughly and came up with nothing. Scanning the area while he finished filling his tank, Zhi didn't spot any suspicious activity or anyone who might be targeting him. "What's your name?"

"Chen Yong from Hubei Province. I'm a simple farmer chasing a dream of better pay and lots of work."

"First, in America, they say family names last, so you are Yong Chen from now on. Now get in the front seat of the car and keep your hands where I can always see them. I will complete a more thorough search later."

"Thank you so much, Mister..."

"Just call me Boss Man, understand?"

"Yes, Boss Man. Thank you, Boss Man."

Yong was now a part of the Cheng Syndicate. Others would find their way to Fairview, and most would regret it.

Chapter 15 – Fairview Chief of Police

OFF STATE ROUTE 58, fifteen minutes north of Fairview, local ranchers drove by a rundown barn but didn't see the two vehicles parked behind it or the two men standing beside them.

"Listen, asshole," said the Fairview police chief, "I let you skate on the possession-for-sale charge with the understanding that you would pay me $50,000 for getting the DA to go along with it. Now you tell me you don't have the money. What the fuck."

"Listen, bro, I'll get you the money. I promise. I just need some time."

Pulling his 9mm out of its holster, Greg Harrison pushed the pistol hard against the man's forehead. "Listen *bro*, you get my money within twenty-four hours, or you'll be a guest at my jail until the money shows up—or a dead man. Your choice, *bro*."

"Yes, sir," he said, shaking from head to foot.

Harrison pushed the little man to the ground, turned his back, and was off in his car before the man got up. For the chief, the encounter had been just another day at the office. Although he had bounced around Oklahoma working for different police departments, he had settled into a routine over the past five years in Fairview. Harrison ruled the city with his authoritative presence and stern demeanor. He was a figure that was both feared and respected within the community.

Rumors about Harrison's questionable practices had circulated for years but were always dismissed as baseless gossip. He had a knack for quashing dissent and maintaining an iron grip on information. However, the arrival of an ambitious journalist was about to change everything.

Emma Parker, a freshly minted reporter from the University of Oklahoma, had no idea what it meant to go after a deeply embedded chief of police. She was just a young, small-town girl who had learned that you would find a story if you let the town talk to you. And so, she had listened in her job at the Fairview Gazette, a small newspaper with a circulation of about three thousand.

The consistent buzz was that the police chief might be embezzling money from the city's coffers. With permission from her boss—the owner of the newspaper, Charlie Simmons—Emma had spent hours at the city treasurer's office, using the Freedom of Information Act to gain access. Fortunately for her, a new hire named Jimmy O'Brien was either interested in helping her or wanted to date her, or both.

He had given her a crash course in the accounting principles of city government, along with a lot of flirting.

As Emma dug through the pile of records, she uncovered inconsistencies with the police department's financial records. She discovered that funds allocated for community projects and police equipment had been siphoned off into obscure accounts controlled solely by the police chief. But what the naive twenty-two-year-old hadn't yet comprehended was that when you started digging, you needed to be careful you weren't digging your own grave.

Leaving behind her investigation for a day to drive out to the country, she was covering a story about a pet dog that had been missing for several months but was found safe five hundred miles away by a caring citizen.

Several miles out of town, she glanced in her mirror and saw a police car close behind her with its lights flashing. She instinctively looked down at her speed and saw she was traveling under the posted speed limit. On these pockmarked gravel roads, you would be crazy to go over thirty-five anyway. She pulled over to let the police car pass, but it stopped behind her, its flashing lights filling her car with reds and blues even though it was the middle of the day.

As the officer approached her car, Emma noticed it was Greg Harrison, the police chief. He had his right hand on his holstered sidearm. Emma began to tremble as she put her window down.

"Registration, driver's license, and proof of insurance, please," he said.

She found the documents and handed them over with shaking hands.

He studied her license before leaning against her car, putting his right arm on the roof and bending down so he was face-to-face with her. "Why, Ms. Emma Parker," he said, his voice dripping with scorn, "don't be nervous. I'm just out here doing my job—if you know what I mean."

She replied in a shaky voice, "Why did you stop me, Chief? I was below the speed limit."

"Well, Miss, you don't have to be speeding to break the law. Your car must also be up to safe standards. Come here, and I'll show you." He moved toward the back bumper.

Emma hesitated, reluctant to leave the safety of her car.

The chief turned and said in a demanding voice, "Get the fuck out of the car, bitch."

She started shaking uncontrollably, scared of what this man might do to her.

"Now!" the chief yelled.

She glanced around. There were no houses, no passersby, no nothing—just her and the chief. She slowly got out of the car.

"Come here and let me show you the problem, Ms. Parker, newspaper reporter."

She walked to the back of the car. "You see here," the chief said, pointing at the brake lens, "it's broken and emitting white light to the rear, which violates Vehicle Code 1164c."

She looked at the perfectly intact red lens and didn't know what to do. She silently prayed that the man wouldn't hurt her.

"Sir, it looks okay to me," she said.

"Well, stupid, look again." With one fast stroke, the chief grabbed his baton and smashed the lens into pieces.

Emma screamed.

"Shut the fuck up, bitch." He'd gotten so close to her that she could smell his cigarette-tainted breath. She started to cry, but he kept talking. "Listen closely. I don't know what you're expecting to find over at the city treasurer's office, but I'll tell you right now—if you fucking keep going over there, then you might be involved in a serious automobile accident with no survivors. Can you picture that, Ms. Emma fucking Parker?"

Emma just cried harder, her mind reeling. She had to get away from this man. She started backing away.

He grabbed her arm and pulled her to within inches of his rage-distorted face. "Say a word about this to anyone, and you can be assured you'll never write another story again." He violently spun her around and pushed her, knocking her to the ground. She felt the gravel rip skin from her knees and hands.

Emma didn't move. She heard the police car's engine roar as he drove within inches of her prone body and sped off. Gravel pelted her face. She lay there crying uncontrollably, her tears making small wet spots on the gravel.

Chapter 16 – Home Grown

As in any successful business enterprise, knowing your customer is essential. Mei Zhao, who had an advanced degree in marketing, did her homework. Her upper-echelon contacts in the Chinese government were more than happy to help because she paid them handsomely. They had been sending her reports on the trending strains of marijuana, consumer preferences, and the best prices to expect for her product. Combining that with the reports of the best grows worldwide, she had her recipe. Marijuana users in the US preferred THC strains—the strains known for their strong psychoactive effects.

In addition, Mei chose strains with stable genetics, which ensured uniform growth, predictable yields, and consistent cannabinoid profiles. Such stability was crucial in maintaining product quality and reliability. After all, she knew that a happy customer was a returning customer.

Getting the seeds from China to the US was not as simple as someone putting them in an envelope, licking a postage stamp, and mailing them. Instead, the seeds were smuggled through various covert methods such as hidden compartments in container shipments and personal transport by Chinese couriers who evaded searches.

As the seeds arrived, Mei oversaw the cultivation process. Her state-of-the-art greenhouses and indoor grow rooms were equipped with high-intensity lighting, climate control systems, and hydroponic setups. She also installed sophisticated irrigation and nutrient delivery systems to ensure optimal plant growth.

As workers arrived almost exclusively from China, Mei selected the most educated to oversee the growth management of the sprouting marijuana plants. The seedlings were carefully monitored through their vegetative and flowering stages. This included precise control of light cycles, temperature, humidity, and nutrient levels. She also ordered the use of fertilizers and pesticides to maximize yields.

Nothing in the grow business was a sprint; everyone had to be reminded that the timeline from planting to distribution was four to six months. But Mei knew they were well on their way to a bumper crop.

WHEN JAKE DALTON MADE a decision, there was no turning back. Some considered it a character flaw, but it was just his way of life. His choice to resign from the LAPD was no exception.

In his heart, Jake knew he had handled the bank robbery response properly and entirely within department policies. To him, the findings were all about politics, plain and simple. Although the police chief was appointed, the mayor and city council made the selection. The previous chief had resigned because of politics, saying he left because, "As chief of police, I could never perform my duties without first answering to my twenty-one bosses. I had fifteen in the city council, five in the police commission, and one in the mayor's office."

Jake knew the current chief was tight with Armstrong and was looking out for his five-year renewal as chief of police, which was coming up in six months. Armstrong was buddies with most of the council members. Such was big-city politics. As a result, it was becoming more difficult for a cop to do his job—Jake was proof of that.

Sick of it all, he figured it was time to get back to his roots in Oklahoma. He was done with the concrete jungle called Los Angeles, so here he sat in his apartment, contemplating whether to call his landlord or his mom first.

A knock at his door interrupted his thoughts. Standing outside was his best friend and partner—make that former partner—Robbie. He was loaded down with a huge box containing all of Jake's items from his locker at the Robbery-Homicide Division.

"Thanks, man, for doing this for me. There was no way I would set foot in that building again."

Robbie let the box drop to the floor, making a big thump as it landed. He grabbed Jake in a big bear hug. "God, how I'm going to miss you."

"I hear ya, buddy, same here for sure."

"Man, I'm so sorry for the way things turned out and even more for fucking this up for you. I know it was a judgment call that day, and I'm sorry I opened my big trap and cast doubt on your decision. I sure didn't want it to go down that way."

Jake gave it a second before pulling away to look him in the eyes. "Robbie, I'll never hold that against you. That's why I get—got—the big bucks. It was a command decision. Those pogues will never get it. I did what I thought was right and will never second-guess how it went down. Shit happens." He slapped Robbie on the shoulder. "Want a beer, partner?"

"Hell yeah." He walked out to the patio and sat while Jake got the beers. "So, have you made any plans?"

Jake joined him, handed over a bottle, then sat and stretched out his legs. "Yep, I'm heading back to Fairview, Oklahoma, where I grew up and where my mom still lives."

Robbie took a pull from his longneck bottle. "What the hell is a gunslinger from LA going to do in bumfuck Oklahoma?"

"Not sure yet. My uncle took over my dad's auto shop, and it's always been understood that I could step in. I started turning wrenches and busting nuts when I was a little kid. I just need to get someone to work the front and handle the admin bullshit; then, I can do my thing with the repairs that come in. You don't get rich, but I couldn't care less about that. It's just a different life and one that's sounding good right now. I sure don't have anything keeping me here."

"I hear you. It just won't be the same without you calling the shots for the unit, though. But life goes on, right?"

"It does. Let's make sure to stay in touch. I care about all the guys from the unit. I'll miss them for sure."

After a couple of beers, the two buds hugged and parted ways. Jake called his landlord, got some boxes, and started packing his stuff. He made arrangements to rent a moving truck that could tow his Porsche. Selling it in LA would give him a nice chunk of change, but there was no way he was saying goodbye to his beautiful lava-orange ride.

After a few days of packing and loading the truck, he was off. Once he left the city limits, he never looked back. He hit the *Alt Nation* channel on satellite radio, which appropriately blasted one of his favorites, the song "All These Things That I've Done" by The Killers. He had soul but was no longer a soldier.

EMMA PARKER DIDN'T show up for work or even call in. She just sat in her small apartment and cuddled with her cat, Roscoe. After getting home from her terrifying encounter with Chief Harrison, she didn't know what to do. Her mind kept replaying how he had threatened to kill her if she talked to anyone. And she believed him. She hadn't slept or eaten, and she could barely function.

Suddenly, her cell phone went off, scaring her so much that she threw Roscoe into the air. He landed with a big shriek, scaring her even more. She was afraid to look to see who was calling, but the phone kept ringing. Eventually, she peeked at the caller ID, then gasped. It was Mr. Simmons from the *Gazette*.

"Hello," she whispered.

"Emma, this is Charlie. What's going on? You sound like you just saw a ghost."

She held the phone to her ear, staring at nothing, not knowing what to do.

"Emma, what the hell's wrong? You're scaring me."

She bit her lip. "Sorry, Mr. Simmons, I'm not—I'm not feeling good. Bye." After ending the call, she found Roscoe and cuddled up with him again, wishing the world would leave her alone.

Back at the *Fairview Gazette*, Charlie sat back in his chair for a moment. Emma had only worked for the paper for three months, but Charlie considered her the child he'd never had. He rushed into the next room, where his wife worked as the paper's accountant.

"Helen, something's wrong with Emma. I just called her, and she seemed really scared."

"Slow down, Charlie. What do you mean?"

"She could barely talk. We need to go see her. Now."

A few minutes later, Charlie knocked on the door of Emma's apartment. No answer. "It's okay, Emma. It's Charlie and Helen. Please answer the door." Again, no answer.

The door opened slightly as he was about to walk around to peek in the windows. Through the crack, he saw Emma. She was pale, her eyes huge and red, and he noticed several small cuts on her cheeks.

Helen stepped in front of her husband. "It's okay, sweetheart, we're here to help you. Please let us in."

The door opened, and Emma retreated inside to Roscoe. She sat on the floor, rocking back and forth with her cat, whimpering. Helen sat on the floor beside her, wrapping an arm around Emma's shoulders and pulling her close.

After a while, Emma told them about the frightening encounter with Chief Harrison. Neither Charlie nor Helen could believe what the young woman had gone through. They also realized that Emma was in grave danger.

Charlie had an idea. He had a close friend with the Oklahoma State Bureau of Investigation, Lieutenant Greg Babbit. He called Babbit and reported the confrontation without missing any details. He also went into the specifics regarding how Emma had uncovered evidence of Harrison embezzling funds from the city.

Babbit listened intently, and immediately dispatched three units to Fairview. He instructed them to obtain a signed crime report of unlawful detention and battery from Ms. Parker and to provide her security even though she would be staying with Charlie and Helen. Babbit then checked the OSBI files and learned that other units within OSBI had been working on a case against Harrison.

The next day, with an arrest warrant in hand, Lieutenant Babbit led a group of four officers to stake out the Fairview Police Department. While Harrison was eating his usual breakfast at Rosie's Diner, Babbit and the three other officers went inside the police station to wait for the chief's

8:30 a.m. arrival. When the chief entered the station, he found himself face-to-face with Babbit.

Babbit pointed his weapon at the chief. "OSBI. Don't take another step or move in any way."

Harrison saw that he was covered by four officers, all with guns pointed at him. Fuck me, he thought.

"Put your hands behind your head now," ordered Babbit. The chief complied instantly. Babbit holstered his weapon, then handcuffed the chief. "You are under arrest for unlawful detention, battery, and bribery. And, I might add, several other charges are also in the works. You have the right to remain silent—"

"Fuck you all!" Harrison interrupted. "I haven't done shit. And the last thing I'm saying to you assholes is that I want an attorney."

At that moment, Charlie popped out from a side room, holding his newspaper's only camera, an old 35mm Nikon. He snapped a picture of the police chief in handcuffs with two uniformed OSBI officers behind him. The front-page photo would make headlines all over rural Oklahoma— headlines read by some interested Chinese Syndicate operatives settling into their new digs in Fairview.

FOR JAKE, PULLING INTO the driveway of his mom's home was like turning the clock back to when he was headed the other way. Back then, he had dreamed of the big city and the LAPD, and now he would just as soon forget the whole thing. He could never forgive the force for turning on him after he'd given them the best years of his life.

Jake had started his life in Fairview, and now it was time to see what was in store for him here. As his mom came out the front door waving, he knew one thing for sure—she would be the rudder that would guide him.

As soon as the rental truck's engine shut off, he was out the door to give his mom a big hug and feel all her love in return. Thank God for Mom, he thought.

"Just look at you," she said with so much excitement that it made his heart sing, "the same as when you left, you handsome son of a gun."

"I bet you still have my room waiting for me, right?"

"Of course, sweetheart. It's your room. Truth be told, though, I did have thoughts of making it my library."

"Well, Mom, this is only temporary until I find a place, so I think your library could be a reality soon."

"Please take your time. I love having you back. It's been so lonely without your dad."

Carrying a suitcase toward the house, Jake said, "I can imagine, after forty-five years together." He felt a lump forming in his throat and decided to get off the subject of loss. "By the way, how's Uncle Joe doing with the shop?"

"He's doing fine. The business is good, and he has a part-time mechanic to help fill in the gaps. He told me he's glad you're coming back home and is anxious to see you."

"I'll get over there tomorrow. I also have to start looking for my own place and catch up with what's happened since I've been gone."

"Well, the biggest news by far is that Police Chief Harrison was arrested a few days ago on a host of charges, including bribery." She grabbed the *Gazette* and showed him the front-page picture.

Jake looked at the picture. The chief was in uniform, staring right into the camera lens with a malicious look. Two OSBI officers flanked him, each holding one of his arms. Jake recognized one of them from years ago.

"Who would have guessed a small-town chief would be so corrupt?" Jake said. "Who's taking his place? Anyone I know?"

"Nobody yet. The remaining four officers are continuing to do their assignments, with oversight by the mayor. The city council will have a special session to see what direction they want to go. My friend Judy from city personnel said they would advertise for a new chief."

"Okay Mom, I need to unpack and then get to town."

"You going to be driving that car of yours?"

"That's a Porsche, and yes, I drive it everywhere. It's my only car. It just doesn't like dirt roads, so I'll have to watch that," he said, smiling.

Jake headed to his room to unpack his luggage. As he went, he caught himself wondering about that chief's position. How weird, he thought.

JAKE OPENED THE DOOR of his Porsche as wide as it would go as his mother aimed her bottom at the seat and fell into it. "Jake, how do you get in and out of this car?"

"I'm a few years younger, Mom."

As he fired up the 340-horsepower mid-engine, he smiled like he always did when he started it. Jake loved the engine's sound so much that he often listened to its hum rather than the upgraded radio because nothing compared to the sound of horsepower. Next, he hit the sport-exhaust button on the console, and the engine purred even louder.

"All set?"

"My, the engine sure is noisy. Your dad drove a truck all his life, and it wasn't nearly as loud."

Jake wasn't going there. Using the paddle shifter for his PDK transmission, he selected first gear, and they were off. Their first stop was for a nice mom-and-son dinner at the town's favorite eating spot, Rosie's.

"Is Rosie still kicking?"

Agnes adjusted herself in the car seat, which felt just inches off the ground and was so unlike the way she used to ride in her husband's truck. "No, she passed two years ago. Her daughter runs it now. Do you know her? Nancy?"

"We were in high school together but hung out with different crowds." Jake had been on the football team and was the most popular kid at Fairview High. Nancy was a quiet kid and pretty much kept to herself. Even back then she worked twenty hours a week at the restaurant.

Pulling up to Rosie's, Jake parked where his Porsche was safe from the score of large pickup trucks surrounding the restaurant.

"Jake, why are we parking so far away?"

"So one of those trucks doesn't door-ding my car. Besides, the exercise is good for ya."

As they walked through the restaurant, several regulars—nearly everyone—said hi to Agnes, who smiled brightly and introduced Jake at each table. Like his mom, Jake knew most of the people, but he noticed how much older they looked.

They sat down at Agnes's usual table, which happened to be open. They noticed an Asian couple at the table next to them. The couple's presence was unusual because the only Asians they knew of in town were those who owned the dry-cleaning business.

A smiling Nancy approached. "Hi, Agnes, nice to see you again. Hi, Jake. It's been a while. How are you doing? Taking a break from the big city?"

"Hi, Nancy," said Agnes with a happy tone.

"Hi," said Jake. "It certainly has been a while. I haven't seen you since I left for LA. I hear you run the place now."

"Sure do. We'll have to catch up sometime. So, what can I get for you two?"

Without looking at the menu, Agnes said, "The regular for me."

"Okay. What vegetable would you like with your meatloaf tonight? Peas or carrots?"

"Hmm...I'll have the carrots."

"Jake?" Nancy asked while scribbling down the order.

"Mom's regular sounds good, but I'll have steak and potatoes since it's been a while."

"Sure. How would you like that cooked?"

"Medium rare, please."

"Will do. It'll be out shortly." As Nancy made her way back to the kitchen, she stopped at the table where the Asian couple was eating and asked if they needed anything. They both thanked her for asking and said the meal was delicious.

As Jake's mom caught him up on the town's happenings, Jake noticed a Fairview police car pull up to the curb outside the restaurant door. A single officer got out and came in. The first thing Jake noticed when he saw the officer was that his uniform looked terrible as if he had slept in it.

Half of his shirt was untucked, and he didn't look clean-shaven.

The officer entered the restaurant, stepped a few feet inside, stopped, and yelled, "Who owns the black Mercedes SUV with temporary plates?"

All conversation ceased. The Asian woman sitting at the table beside Jake's half-raised her hand. "I do, Officer."

The sloppy officer charged over to their table. "Do you know you're blocking the entrance to Joe's Barbershop?"

"I am so sorry," said the woman. "We saw that the business was closed for the night and parked there since there was no room elsewhere."

"Listen, I don't know where you two come from, but around here, you just don't park anywhere you want to. Do I make myself clear?"

Jake couldn't take the officer's attitude any longer and stood up. "Officer, may I suggest you have them move their car so we can all return to our meals and conversations?"

The officer spun toward Jake, "Excuse me? I suggest you shut up and sit down before you get yourself in trouble. This has nothing to do with you."

"Well, it does, Officer," said a pissed-off Jake. "You don't need to read the riot act to these customers while we're all trying to eat. Just have them move the car, and you might try doing it politely."

The officer walked over and stood right in front of Jake. He had to tilt his head up to look Jake in the eyes. "Listen, partner, one more word out of you and I'll arrest you for interfering with an official police investigation."

As the officer concentrated on Jake, the Asian woman got up and walked around him, heading for the door.

The officer turned away from Jake. "Wait a minute, lady. Where do you think you're going?"

"To move my car, Officer."

"I'll tell you when you can leave. Sit back down."

She complied.

"Whoa, Officer," said Jake, "you're blowing this way out of proportion. I would like to talk with your supervisor."

"Well, guess what, dipshit? How about I haul your ass over to the city jail, and you talk to him from a jail cell when he comes to work tomorrow?"

From the other corner of the room, a man approached the officer. "Stop it right now, Officer Thomas. What in the world are you doing?"

Officer Thomas saw the mayor. Shit, he thought. He quickly changed his demeanor and looked like a pet dog that had just been caught eating its owner's best shoe. "Sorry,

Mr. Mayor. I was asking these people to move their car when this smart-ass—excuse me, this man—began interfering with my investigation."

"Interfering? You're lucky this LA cop didn't kick your ass, which he would have had every right to do."

Officer Thomas looked over at Jake. "Sorry, sir."

"Report to the station immediately," the mayor said to Officer Thomas. "I'll be there after I eat my now-cold meal. Get out of here."

Thomas was gone just as fast as he had entered. The mayor turned to the Asian couple and said, "I'm so sorry for the behavior of one of my town's police officers. Where you're parked is just fine. In fact, it's my go-to place when Rosie's lot is overflowing."

"Thank you," said the woman sheepishly. We didn't mean to cause all this trouble."

"You didn't do anything wrong. I'll handle this matter, and again, I'm very sorry for Officer Thomas's actions."

The mayor turned to Agnes. "Hi, Agnes." Then he looked at Jake. "Nice to see you again, Jake. Sorry about that, but since the chief was arrested, the department's remaining officers think they can do as they please. We hope to have a new chief shortly. Good to see you back in Fairview."

The mayor returned to his seat, and the restaurant soon buzzed with conversations. As for Jake, he had other thoughts and didn't eat much of his meal.

Chapter 21 – The Meeting

A FEW DAYS AFTER the incident at Rosie's, Jake set up a meeting with Mayor Richard Waterhouse because he was troubled by Officer Thomas's actions and couldn't stop thinking about them. How an officer could be so obnoxious and berate that woman in front of all those people was simply unacceptable, no matter the size of the city or the department.

Jake had thought he would be done with public service after leaving the LAPD, that he was ready to return to civilian life and take over his dad's auto repair business. But the more he thought about it, the more he realized he had loved being a cop more than anything else in his life—not so much the serving part, but the putting bad people in jail part. It was the game he missed, the one that had been going on since the first lawman walked his first beat, with criminals trying to outsmart him. There was something special about outwitting some asshole and throwing him in jail, something that civilians would never comprehend. He also loved the job for its camaraderie.

Entering the mayor's small office in the town's dated city hall, Jake realized he had only known of the mayor while growing up and didn't really know him. Jake had no opinion about the man other than an appreciation of how he had handled the incident at Rosie's.

"Welcome, Jake," said the mayor from behind his desk. "It's nice to see you back in Fairview, and from what I hear on the street, you'll be staying."

Jake chuckled at the statement. "Thanks, Mayor Waterhouse. You sure can't hide anything from anybody in this town. But then, the ex-chief of police learned that the hard way."

The mayor smiled at that and motioned to a chair in front of his desk. "Please call me Richard. So, what can I do for you?"

"Just to set the record straight," Jake said as he took a seat, "I resigned from the LAPD for political reasons and for the second-guessing that is now ingrained in that department. I was a supervisor, a ten-year model cop who got into a righteous shooting in a bank and killed the main suspect, who was holding a hostage. All of it was justified. But let's just say some people wanted to nitpick elements of what happened before the robbery, for retaliation and vindictiveness because of an arrest I'd made years ago. So I decided the big city wasn't for me anymore."

Jake sat up even straighter. "Since that embarrassing situation at Rosie's the other night, I've thought long and hard, and I would like to apply for the position of chief of police. I feel I bring a lot to the table, and even though the police department is only the chief and four officers, I can make the Fairview PD a quality and respected outfit. As you know, I grew up here and have a lot of respect for the town's hardworking citizens. I want a chance to change their perceptions of the department."

The mayor paused before saying, "Jake, I was worried you would never ask. I agree with what you've said and believe you would be a perfect fit. You came back at just the right time. I'll close the position advertisement and let the city council know my choice. The council will still need to vote on it, but with my recommendation, you can plan on being sworn in within a week. The city clerk will review all the particulars, but I estimate your annual salary to be $48,000."

"Sounds perfect. I'm looking forward to getting started. If anyone has a question, problem, or comment, we can meet with them to take care of it rather than letting it simmer. I guess in today's world, they call it transparency. And I will always keep you up to date on anything I believe you will have an interest in."

Jake walked out the door as the next chief of police. He couldn't wait to start his new life.

Chapter 22 – The Start of Something Big

IN A SMALL TOWN like Fairview, if you did anything out of the ordinary, you'd better have an explanation because people would ask. Not even the town realtor was exempt. You could be in the cereal aisle at the grocery store deciding between cornflakes and raisin bran, and someone might stop you with "Hey George, I heard you—" and you never had any idea what would follow. Now that he was the representative for his newfound Chinese friends, he had to have a rock-solid story to get past those prying questions. There were no secrets in Fairview, so he just added one more thing to his BS portfolio.

George had been practicing his elevator speech in case anyone approached him asking about the marijuana business. He decided he would thank them for asking and say that as a veteran real estate broker and an investor with a large portfolio of properties, he'd heard about the investment possibilities of the newly legal cannabis-growing business and had jumped at the chance to be a lead investor. He would add how excited he was about the new opportunity, a method of covertly shaming the person from saying anything bad about it.

George now used his pitch not just in the cereal aisle but all over town and beyond, like when he registered Green Horizon Cultivation LLC with the State of Oklahoma for the legal cultivation and sale of marijuana. When he registered with the Oklahoma Medical Marijuana Authority, they were much more stringent. OMMA required proof of financial solvency and proof of two years of state residency, and then George had to pass a background check.

Once George had completed all the administrative work, two Chinese companies with ties to the syndicate shipped 440,000 pounds of greenhouse parts to Fairview, to build over one hundred greenhouses and leave enough material for several indoor grow houses. In addition, they sent specialty crews with legal credentials to construct the buildings and install state-of-the-art security. A few buildings were glass-enclosed greenhouses, built to the state's specs for legal growth operations and positioned at the front of the property. The rest were located far from the legal greenhouses and concealed what was inside. Care was taken to ensure the cover buildings had state-mandated ventilation systems and adhered to all local statutes.

Once construction was complete, George was required to maintain proper records, submit to inspections, and follow state guidelines for product quality. He considered such responsibilities no problem at all. And he knew if things got too sticky, he could ask for more money to get unstuck. He'd learned that the pockets of his employers were deep.

As the LLC's on-site leader, Li prioritized security. His goal was to protect the operation from outside threats, such as law enforcement and rival criminal groups, while maintaining the secrecy of the illegal activities. To keep a low profile but still maintain tight security, he had thermal imaging cameras installed near all the greenhouses, making it difficult for intruders to approach unnoticed, even in low-visibility conditions like nighttime or fog.

He also installed microwave beams to create an invisible detection field around the perimeters of the greenhouse areas. The system had several advantages. When an object or person disrupted the beam, it triggered an alarm. The system was effective over long distances and completely hidden from view. It was also backed up by laser systems which created invisible boundaries by projecting laser beams across other areas. If someone crossed a beam, it triggered an alert.

Finally, Li emplaced ground vibration sensors to detect pulsations caused by footsteps, vehicles, or digging. He buried them underground and connected them to an alarm system that would alert his security personnel to any disturbances near the property lines.

Li felt confident in all aspects of the build. He felt the show George was putting on for the town would keep suspicious eyes away from the illegal aspect of the operation that was positioned deep inside the property. The complexity and thoroughness of his concealment strategies would make it extremely difficult for law enforcement, especially the Fairview PD, to uncover the full extent of their activities.

Chapter 23 – The New Chief of Police

Since it was built in the early 1900s, the Fairview town hall has hosted many special occasions in the small auditorium at the back of the building. Not much had been done to the one-story building over the years because the town's growth remained stable, but it served its purpose throughout time. Today would add to its history.

The Fairview Women's Club had spruced things up by placing an American flag and the Oklahoma state flag in the middle of the stage as a backdrop for the podium, which was adorned with the city's seal. Flanking the rostrum were chairs for the town's dignitaries, including the mayor and the town council. In the back of the auditorium, several tables were packed with lemonade, iced tea, water, coffee, homemade brownies, cookies, and cakes.

Jake was offstage with his four officers—who would soon be three, although Officer Thomas didn't know it yet. They had a new look, thanks to Jake. Instead of their old tan uniforms, they now wore navy blue uniforms adorned with metal buttons. They soon would have Fairview Police Department patches sewn onto their upper sleeves. Badges similar to the LAPD's were on order. Jake had loved his old badge, and since the LAPD had let the copyright expire, any department could use the design. The oval-shaped badge's centerpiece would be an artist's rendering of the statue of Arthur Fairview, the town's founder, with POLICE OFFICER in blue lettering at the top, CITY OF FAIRVIEW below the statue, and the officer's badge number at the bottom. Jake's badge would differ by saying CHIEF instead of OFFICER, and he chose 2235—his LAPD number—as his badge number. The other officers would have sequential numbers after his. He'd gotten a lot done in the week following his meeting with the mayor.

As Jake peeked through the curtains, he saw people come in and take their seats—all the local politicians, the county sheriff, his mom with her friends, and several local business owners, including Nancy from Rosie's, and Charlie and Helen Simmons from the newspaper. Emma Parker sat with Charlie and Helen and looked much better now. He also saw the Asian woman from Rosie's. She was with realtor George Sullivan.

The room grew quiet, the typical signal that the meeting was about to start. Jake was calm and even comfortable, looking forward to the challenges that lay ahead. Jake led his four officers onto the stage, sitting alongside the mayor.

As Mayor Waterhouse went to the podium, he took a moment to get everyone's attention, then started the ceremony.

Good afternoon, everyone. Thank you for joining us today for this important occasion. As mayor of Fairview, it is both an honor and a responsibility to ensure that our town remains a safe and welcoming place for all. A big part of that responsibility is choosing the right leadership for our police department, and I'm proud to introduce our new chief of police, Jake Dalton.

When it came time to select our new chief, I knew we needed someone with experience and skill, a deep understanding of our community, and a commitment to its well-being. Fairview is more than just a town. It's a place where neighbors look out for one another, where families have lived for generations, and where we pride ourselves on maintaining the values that make this community special.

Jake Dalton embodies those values. With over ten years of law enforcement experience, and having earned the prestigious Medal of Valor from the Los Angeles Police Department, Jake has demonstrated time and again his dedication to upholding the law and to protecting those he serves. But more than that, Jake understands the unique challenges we face in Fairview and the importance of building trust between the police department and the citizens it serves.

Throughout his career, Jake has shown a remarkable ability to connect with people from all walks of life, to listen to their concerns, and to lead with integrity and fairness. These qualities are essential in a police chief, and I do not doubt that Jake will continue to foster the strong relationships that are the cornerstone of effective community policing.

In selecting Jake Dalton as our new police chief, we are choosing a leader who is not only capable and qualified but who also cares deeply about this town and its people. I'm confident that under Jake's leadership, our police department will continue to be a force for good, ensuring that Fairview remains the safe and vibrant community we all cherish.

So please join me in welcoming Jake Dalton as Fairview's new chief of police. I know he will serve us well, and I look forward to all he will accomplish in this new role. Chief.

Jake came from stage right, smiled at the crowd, shook the mayor's hand, and thanked him. The mayor took a seat on the stage, and Jake stood behind the podium.

Thank you, Mayor Waterhouse, for those kind words, and thank you to everyone here today for your trust and support. It's an incredible honor to be standing here as the new chief of police for Fairview, a town I've grown up in, known, and loved over the years.

When I first started in law enforcement, I did so because I believed in the importance of service—service to the community, to the people, and to the values that make our society strong. Throughout my career, that belief has only grown more robust, and today, I'm more committed than ever to upholding those principles here in Fairview.

I want to lead a department that not only enforces the law but also builds bridges of trust and respect with the community. To me, effective policing isn't just about responding to incidents. It's about being proactive, engaging with residents, understanding their concerns, and working together to find solutions. I believe transparency, accountability, and open communication are key to achieving this.

In the days ahead, I plan to meet with as many of you as possible to learn about you and your concerns and to share my vision for how we can continue to make Fairview a model of community policing. I'm committed to working closely with our officers and ensuring they have the tools, training, and support they need to do their jobs effectively and safely.

I also want to take a moment to thank my family, my fellow officers, and everyone who has supported me along the way. Your encouragement and belief in me mean the world, and I wouldn't be here without you.

I know there are challenges ahead, but I'm confident we can face them together and continue building a community where everyone feels safe, respected, and valued.

After the applause ended, the town judge and Jake's mother came forward. She held the 150-year-old family Bible for her son to place his right hand on as he took the oath of office. When they finished, the mayor pinned on the soon-to-be-replaced FPD badge and shook Jake's hand again.

After the ceremonies, the mayor turned to the crowd and said, "Okay, let's enjoy the wonderful desserts and drinks provided by the Women's Club."

Sitting in the crowd, Mei wondered if this Jake man would impact their operations. She didn't think so, but he looked like he could be an impediment with his big-city police experience. Even with that, though, he would be no match against the syndicate that supported her—the Cheng Syndicate—one of China's most powerful criminal organizations.

JAKE HAD A RENEWED love for his profession. Now wearing a star on his collar, he was determined to serve Fairview with the finest small police department in Oklahoma. As the chief, he understood that he needed training in that position to lead his officers to be their best. He had the mayor and city council agree to fund the dues for his acceptance into the International Chiefs of Police Association. It was the top organization for police chiefs from around the world, and the association's mission was to advance the policing profession through advocacy, research, education, and the development of best practices for city policing.

As he had promised, Jake spent his first week interviewing each of his four officers. First up was Officer Thomas, and it wouldn't be a pleasant affair.

Thomas sauntered into Jake's office in civilian clothes, and even those were messy and wrinkled. Jake didn't bother to offer him a seat.

"Thomas, I know this is your day off, so I'll cut right to the chase, as it seems that's your style. You're fired. I want your badge, your firearm, and all city keys you have. Any questions?"

"You're such a prick. You come back to town like you own it. Well, let me be the first to tell you, you don't own shit. And another thing, I came here to quit. I have a better job that pays three times as much. You can take your new badges and stick them up your ass." Thomas stormed out.

After the station's door slammed shut, Jake hollered to his office administrator and lead gossip hound. "Mary, have you heard where Thomas got hired?"

"Yes, Chief, I got a call from Green Horizon Cultivation, the new marijuana farm in town. They asked if I could give a referral for Thomas because they were considering hiring him. I told them to call you, which I guess they didn't do. If I may speak frankly, that man has always been a jerk, and I about died when the previous chief hired him. He and Harrison seemed to be buds instead of having a chief-and-subordinate relationship."

"Okay, Mary, thanks. I appreciate the intel. I believe Thomas just made it onto my radar. Please ensure we get the ad out for his replacement, and keep me posted on any applications. And let me know when Thomas turns his stuff in, too."

"Will do, Chief."

During the next week, between getting out and about in the community to introduce himself to the townspeople, Jake interviewed his three remaining officers. None had prior police experience, which was about what he expected for a small-town department. That was fine with him. From his days in the LAPD, he knew that probationary officers out of the Academy were as good or as bad as their training officers. A lazy, do-nothing training officer usually resulted in a similar recruit. On the other hand, a sharp training officer usually turned out an above-average officer. With Jake as their training officer, his officers would be molded in a way that complemented their backgrounds and would turn them into positive, community-oriented officers who could get the job done.

One of his three remaining officers was two-year officer Billy Ray Weber, a forty-two-year-old former long-haul truck driver who had quit driving to spend more time with his wife and eight-year-old son. He grew up in a rural area near Fairview and knew the residents quite well. Although still learning and a little rough around the edges—which Jake would iron out—he was reliable and practical. He loved the new badge Jake had designed and had put it on his uniform with a proud smile.

Jake's next interview was with Joe Clarkson, the youngest of the group. Joe Clarkson was a twenty-nine-year-old lifelong resident of Fairview who had worked at the family grocery store until he saw the ad for a Fairview police officer. He'd been ready for a change. The kid knew everyone in town by their first name, was very popular in the community, and was a fair-minded officer who liked resolving issues with calm conversation rather than by using force.

Number three was a handful from the time she was born. Emily "Em" Carter was a thirty-year-old firecracker who grew up on a cattle ranch just outside of Fairview. She was raised by her single father, a no-nonsense rancher, and had learned to ride, rope, and take care of animals by working alongside the ranch hands and proving herself every step of the way. She would never back down from a challenge, whether taming a stubborn horse or fixing a broken-down tractor in the middle of a storm.

At the end of Jake's interview, she said, "Look, Chief, I appreciate what you may have done in LA, but this isn't the big city. These are hardworking, blue-collar people who don't want any bullshit. They only want the truth. Just thought you should know." She got up and left.

As Em went out the front door, Mary knew the chief would call her in on this one.

"Mary, can you come here a minute?" said the chief, right on cue.

"Coming, Chief."

"Wow, that girl is sure wired tight," Jake said as Mary entered his office. "How is she doing out on the streets?"

Mary smiled. "I've known the family forever, and Em since she was a kid. I watched her grow up competing in rodeos, arguing with the head football coach because she wanted to play on the team, and recently deciding to leave the family business because she wanted to be a Fairview police officer. Despite her short time on the force, she has earned a reputation as a hard-ass who doesn't take any bullshit. Em has a Type A personality and is ambitious, competitive, and always striving for perfection. She's the first to arrive at work and the last to leave, takes the toughest assignments and pushes herself to be the best. Most of us respect her, though some find her intensity a bit overwhelming. Her biggest challenge is learning to be part of a team she's not in charge of. Good luck with her, but I'll tell you, I love that girl. She reminds me of myself back in the day."

"Well, I must admit, I sure didn't expect to see that type of officer being part of our small department. But she's my type of cop. She just needs to have her rough edges smoothed over."

IT HAD BEEN A couple of months since Samantha Taylor had contacted Jake. Right after the robbery, she'd had nightmares of being thrown into the back seat of the bank robber's car and then being chased by a line of police cars. As she was thrown around in the robber's car, she got a glimpse of the driver, who wasn't the bank robber but some monster-looking thing. Not that it made any sense, but her visions wouldn't stop. It had gotten to the point that she was scared to go to bed—until that breakfast with Jake.

She didn't know what to call their relationship or even if that was the right word. Whatever it was, being around Jake for that short time had made her feel safe and protected, and the nightmares began to fade. However, as the weeks passed, the bad dreams returned, so she wanted to talk with Jake again and, she hoped, see him. She thought he would understand and might be able to help her.

Sam dialed the only number she had: his work number.

"Robbery-Homicide Division, Fugitive Detail," said a flat voice displaying no emotion.

"Hello, may I please talk with Detective Dalton? This is Samantha Taylor."

There was a pause on the other end, which immediately made her feel uncomfortable, as if something terrible had happened. "Is this Ms. Taylor from the bank robbery?" said a vaguely familiar voice.

Now, she was scared. Something didn't seem right.

"Yes," she said, "is there something wrong?"

"Ma'am, this is Detective Robinson, Jake's old partner. He resigned from the LAPD."

What? Sam thought. Jake hadn't indicated he was resigning. True, they'd never spoken again after that breakfast, and they hadn't been at a point where they would share things like that, but still, quitting seemed so unlike the man who hadn't given up on her in the bank.

Robbie, sensing this, considered how much he should tell her. The line was silent. Finally, he said, "Ms. Taylor, we have to be tight-lipped here at LAPD for many reasons, but since I know you and what you've been through, I'll let Jake know you called. That's all I can do. Okay?"

"Sorry, detective, I'm just so surprised by—"

"Ms. Taylor, I can't say anything else. I'll contact him, but please don't call back if he doesn't call you. You have my word that I'll reach out to him. Goodbye."

Robbie hung up and wondered what Jake would want. He'd left LAPD by choice, and he hadn't called the hostage since. Those were his choices and his business—no one else's, especially not the hostage's. If he shined this off, Jake would never know that she called, and she would never know that he hadn't called Jake. End of subject. Life moves on.

But then Robbie flashed back to that day in the bank: the blood splattered all over the woman and dead people on the floor. She was one brave SOB, and fuck it—he owed it to her to do what he promised, and let fate take it from there.

He still had Jake on auto-dial. Doing the math, he figured it was 4:00 p.m. in Oklahoma. Shit, it was so weird that Jake was in Oklahoma.

Jake was at his desk working on the department's training program when his phone rang. Looking down at his caller ID, he saw it was Robbie. That was weird. He didn't think he would hear from him again, or at least not for a while. He picked up on the first ring.

"My man," Robbie said, "how they hangin', dude?"

"Shit, Robbie, I sure didn't think I would hear from you so soon. Are you looking for a new job, or just missing me?"

"Well, buddy, there's some business, if you must know. I just hung up the phone here at work, and it was Samantha Taylor, the hostage lady."

That was strange, thought Jake. He'd left all that baggage in LA to move on with a clean slate. He'd never even told her he'd left the LAPD. "Did she say what she wanted?"

"No, but she sounded upset with the news that you resigned. Look, buddy, I debated even telling you, but I have a soft spot for that girl. She went through so much from that asshole Rawlins, so I dropped a dime to you. Do you have her number?"

No, he didn't, and why would he? She was a victim, and he didn't collect those numbers. "I don't have it. What is it? Maybe I'll call her." Robbie relayed the number, and Jake wrote it on his messy desk blotter.

"Okay, buddy," Robbie said. "Congratulations again on being numero uno in Fairview fucking Oklahoma. Do you even have any crime? Or is the big caper a felony warrant for a runway cat?" Robbie laughed at his joke. "Seriously, though, take care, buddy. Stay in touch." The call ended.

Jake got up from his desk to check with Mary about some training materials he'd ordered. He left behind the phone number jotted down without a name next to it, forgotten like the city he'd left.

Chapter 26 – Workers

To run a marijuana operation in the US, the last thing you needed was Americans working it, thought Mei. Most were lazy people who constantly demanded higher pay, and they talked too much. Mei knew from experience that she needed hardworking Chinese people who owed their very existence to her and the Cheng Syndicate. Using the syndicate's extensive network, the recruiters targeted people in underprivileged regions by promising the poor suckers well-paying jobs abroad. The pledge of high earnings, coupled with the allure of the American dream, was all that was needed to persuade those individuals to take a risk.

Chinese government officials who helped spread the word and obtained forged documents for top prospects to fly into the US were also on the syndicate's payroll. However, most workers had to use the hazardous route that Yong Chen had taken through Mexico. For the Chinese criminals operating in the US, there was always a steady stream to pick from.

Mei had fifty workers running the large-scale operation. As they arrived—dirty, worn out, and broken—Mei made it clear that either they produced or she would dump them back in Mexico. And if they became a threat to the operation, she would shoot them. It was their choice.

Mei interviewed every person who came in, slotting them into positions appropriate for their abilities. The jobs were plentiful. She needed cultivators, trimmers, security details, drivers, pest controllers, nutrient managers, environmental monitors, and kitchen and maintenance staff.

The large barn on their property was converted to living quarters for the workers, including a bathroom and kitchen. She made Yong her assistant to supervise the workers and look for any trouble that might develop. She found the farmer helpful, always there for her and doing whatever she requested. As the time for harvest grew nearer, everything was in place. Then the city inspector showed up.

FRANKIE HAD SAT AT the same desk for twelve years. It was in the heart of a large office that housed the bureaucratic infrastructure a city was required to have in order to function. The pay sucked, and the job was just okay. His desk nameplate read:

Inspector Frank Porter

Building & Safety

He was the chief inspector. There were no others.

From sitting behind his desk most of the time, his once athletic body was giving way to age and his I-don't-give-a-shit-what-I-eat attitude. Drinking every night probably didn't help. Framed by thinning brown hair, his round face had a perpetual five o'clock shadow. He wore a uniform of his own creation: rumpled khakis and a plaid shirt with a pocket for his notebook, the shirt a different color for each day of the week.

Frankie was a fixture in Fairview. Born and raised there, he'd followed in his father's footsteps by entering public service, though he'd chosen the path of building inspector rather than law enforcement. His father, a decorated police officer, had always pushed him toward something "respectable." Frankie's decision to be an inspector was a way of staying close to the family legacy without the risks and confrontation of police work. He hated confrontations of any kind.

In the beginning, Frankie had approached his job with a sense of duty, believing in his heart that his role was vital to keeping Fairview safe and orderly. However, years of dealing with bureaucratic red tape, budget cuts, and the apathy of his superiors and the town's residents had worn him down. His idealism had faded to a quiet resentment of the system and a desire for something more out of life—something the small town of Fairview couldn't offer.

Frankie was pragmatic to a fault. He knew and played the game well, understanding that sometimes bending the rules was necessary to get things done. This practicality made him susceptible to petty corruption, especially when he realized there was no other way to improve his situation. But deep down, Frankie was conflicted. He knew the small bribes were wrong, but the prospect of easy money and a more comfortable life for his family of four had dulled his conscience.

Today was going to be a big day in Frankie's life. He knew it because of all the recent traffic around his desk. The mayor and several city council members had stopped by his desk, supposedly to chitchat—which they never did—but to deliver a subtle message. It went something like this: "The new marijuana-grow business is a big deal for the city. The tax revenues alone will add substantially to a depleted city budget. Frankie, please work with them and iron out any issues while you're there. We want everyone to be happy."

But Frankie had his own ideas.

Driving his city truck down an unmarked access road, he approached a substantial Victorian home. George Sullivan stood on the front porch. Frankie knew George had something to do with the business because his name was on all the permits.

George greeted Frankie with a firm handshake and his usual big smile. Frankie thought he was all bullshit, but he had his orders and made nice.

After several minutes of small talk, George pointed to a fancy golf cart, and the two headed down a nondescript gravel road. After a short time, they arrived at the first of many large greenhouses neatly arranged in a stacked formation—one behind the next. Frankie counted ten of them.

George walked Frankie to the main entrance, continuing to make small talk and not discussing anything related to the buildings. As they entered the greenhouse, the first thing that hit Frankie was a strong, earthy odor. George explained how the grow operation would help Oklahoma with its perpetual shortage of medical-grade marijuana.

Frankie noticed the inside of the building was clean but industrial-looking, with row after row of healthy-looking green plants under bright lights. Chinese workers moved methodically between the rows, tending to the plants and never making eye contact with him. The setup was sophisticated, with high-tech irrigation and ventilation systems, and security cameras that Frankie knew were recording their every move.

Frankie raised his clipboard and pen, which showed he was in charge and diminished any power the business owners thought they had over him. It was a move that he thoroughly enjoyed no matter how many times he had done it—and he was careful never to show how much so. Frankie made notes and checked boxes as they walked down the long aisles. He caught George looking over his shoulder, and the cheesy grin the realtor always wore faded as if he'd just been caught cheating on a math test.

Frankie put on his show but didn't look too closely at the plants or ask probing questions. He was there to do his job on paper, not to find anything. As the inspection wrapped up, George led Frankie back to the office, a small room with a desk and a couple of chairs. He offered Frankie a cold water bottle and then sat behind the desk.

Leaning back in his chair, George said, "We appreciate you coming out here today, Frankie. We're trying to keep everything transparent, you know, to make sure we're not stepping on any toes."

He let his words hang in the air as he reached into a drawer, pulled out a thick white envelope, and pushed it across the desk toward Frankie. Staring at it momentarily, Frankie picked it up, the weight of the envelope a tangible reminder of the decision he was making. But the thought of his bills, his family, and the possibility of a better life outweighed any doubts. Frankie peeked inside the envelope and saw a row of crisp $100 bills—more money than he'd seen in one place in a long time. But it wasn't an obscene amount, and he understood it was just enough to clarify that this was a first payment. He slid the envelope into his jacket pocket without saying a word.

THE HUANG SISTERS—FEN and Qiu—had discussed it whenever they could, which meant late at night in the sisters' hut in Xiaogang, a small farming town in China. They knew their widowed mom needed them to work the fields, but a man in the village had told them they could make much more money in the United States. They reasoned they would be fools not to take advantage of such an opportunity; they could make the trip and send money back to their mom. By leaving, they could support her more than they could by staying here.

Fen, the lifelong self-appointed protector of her little sister Qiu, was skeptical about their source of information. At nineteen, she had learned not to trust anyone, especially men. People often had motives other than what was presented. But Qiu's endless optimism focused only on the promise of a better life. She pointed out their dire situation and that their life would never change if they stayed in their village.

Eventually, Qiu persuaded Fen to take the chance. They borrowed money from their friends and an aunt—people who had little more in life than their mom had. The sisters said they would repay everyone when they made it rich in America.

After a harrowing and dangerous journey to the US, the two girls arrived in Fairview, Oklahoma, broke and with high hopes for the good life. However, it wasn't long before the truth became clear.

Li Cheng, who controlled the marijuana-grow operation, had other plans for the two sisters. Li told them they could repay their debts faster by attending Li's social events and entertaining his guests. Fen and Qiu jumped at the chance to make more money, and they began serving drinks and dancing for Li's numerous male friends. But over time, the sisters were forced into prostitution. They were told that if they didn't perform, Li would kill their family members back in Xiaogang and turn the two of them over to immigration authorities. Fen and Qiu knew that would mean deportation back to their village in China and living the rest of their lives in shame.

Fen, who had always protected her little sister, felt an overwhelming sense of guilt and failure. She'd promised to take care of Qiu, but instead, they were trapped in a nightmare from which there seemed to be no escape. The sisters were constantly watched, and the Cheng Syndicate's enforcers controlled their every move. One slip-up meant harm to their family back in China.

The sisters had no freedom. To further ensure their compliance, Li periodically beat them to remind them who the boss was and to whom they should obey. Not long after arriving with dreams of finally being self-sufficient with money in their pockets, both sisters suffered from depression, anxiety, and a deep sense of hopelessness. Thoughts of escaping from Li pushed out every other thought they had.

Chapter 29 – The Phone Number

As Jake reviewed the record of his first hire, he was happy with his eclectic mix of officers—there was something for everyone. The new officer was Robert "Bob" Spectrum. He had recently retired from the Marine Corps as a first sergeant and wanted to stay busy, feeling too young to be put out to pasture. The forty-year-old had been an MP, so his experience would add much to the force.

His knowledge had also allowed him to test for the position without attending a police academy, and he passed with high marks, so Jake immediately issued him his badge and two uniforms. On the Fairview PD, officers could use a sidearm of their choice, within reason, and since Bob had an acceptable sidearm, Jake put him into the shift rotation right away. Last night, on Bob's first shift, Jake had ridden with him to show him around. On tonight's shift, he had scheduled Bob to ride with Em, figuring that would be a good test for the rookie officer.

As Jake filed Bob's record in a drawer, he decided to get the rest of the paperwork off his desk and into the appropriate files. In the middle of that project, he noticed a phone number scratched on his desk blotter. After staring at it briefly, he remembered who it belonged to—Sam.

Jake wondered why she was contacting him again. He got it, her being a hostage and him saving her life, but her holding his hand at breakfast had been...interesting, to say the least. But that didn't mean he had feelings for the girl. He had hardly ever dated. His relationship with the job took priority. When off duty, he enjoyed reading and going for walks, but mainly, he liked just being alone. On the few dates he'd had, the girls seemed too out there, difficult to figure out, and confusing. He hadn't ever loved anyone except family.

As he was thinking, he unconsciously drew circles around the phone number. Now, he switched to abstract marks as he debated the pros and cons of calling her. He was used to quickly making life-and-death decisions while chasing felons all over LA, or just taking some time to make the right decisions for more routine life and work matters. But this decision seemed different, much more complicated.

Let's see, he thought, if I don't call her, I will move on, and things will be no different. If I call and chat for a few minutes, I can let her know I'm busy and we both need to move on from what happened at the bank. Or I can talk with her and see where it goes, what she wants, that sort of thing.

He tossed his pen onto the desk.

He knew that no matter what happened, he respected the hell out of her. Instead of just being another victim, she'd fought back and won, which counted for a lot in his world.

He decided to make one last call. Glancing at his watch, he calculated the two-hour time difference and figured calling her at 7:00 a.m. in LA would catch her before she left for work. The second after he dialed, he realized that she would now have his cell number, and he mentally kicked himself for not using the department's landline.

"Hello," she said after two rings.

"Hi Sam, it's Jake. I heard—"

"Thank you so much for calling. You have no idea what this means to me."

She sounded excited, which was different from how calm she'd been when she had a gun pointed at her head. Stick to the facts, Jake told himself.

"My former partner, Robbie, let me know you'd called. So, what's up, Sam?"

"First off, when I called your LAPD number, they told me you'd resigned from the force. It surprised me."

"I did, but that's another story. I don't really want to discuss it."

"I understand. I wasn't trying to pry."

Not sure how to read this call, Jake said, "So what's up? I'm not involved with your case anymore."

"I have to level with you."

Okay, here it comes, he thought.

"That day at the bank," she said, "when I thought I could be dead any second, you suddenly arrived and saved my life. Well, I get confusing thoughts about you." She paused, but he didn't interrupt her. "I didn't tell you, but I had nightmares after the bank incident. Then, after we met for breakfast, my nightmares disappeared, and I slept fine for a while. But now the nightmares are back, and I get them every night. I'm struggling with all this. I want to see you again."

There was a long silence while Jake thought about how to answer. This wasn't a robbery in progress, which he could handle in his sleep. It was a woman crying for help, a situation not taught in the academy.

"Jake?"

"Sorry," he said, still at a loss for words.

"I feel like I can open up to you. If I'm wrong, then tell me, and I'll never call you again."

Jake stopped overthinking the situation and quickly replied, "No, it's good you called, and I feel bad for you. I should have let you know that I left the LAPD. I now live in

Fairview, Oklahoma, which is my hometown. I'm the town's police chief."

"Good for you. Listen, I'm thinking off the top of my head now, but I have a convention in New York City next week and would enjoy seeing you on my return trip. What do you think?"

"Wow, you caught me off guard on that one," said Jake. "Text me the details, and I'll see what I can do."

"Thanks. I promise not to be a pest. It's just that I felt better after we talked, and I want to get through all of this. You can certainly help that process."

"Okay, you have my number, so I'll look for your text. Take care and we'll talk later." He quickly ended the call before anything else came out.

Women, Jake thought, I'll never figure them out.

As two of the four officers from Fairview PD drove down Washington Street in the same car, they were turning heads. Citizens couldn't recall when they last saw two officers in the same patrol vehicle when one wasn't the police chief. Some couldn't resist and waved them down to discover what was happening.

"Hey, Em," asked one person, "what gives? We have four officers on the entire police force, and now two of you are cruising together. What's the hitch? Got a big raid going on?"

"New chief, new rules," Em said with a straight face as she kept her hands on the steering wheel. "Okay, Fred," she smiled after seeing the man's eyes widen, "I'm BS-ing you. This is our newest addition," she said, nodding over to the passenger, "Bob Spectrum, who just retired after twenty years in the Marine Corps Military Police."

"Damn, that's impressive. Thank you, sir, for your service. But I have to question your choice of partners," Fred said with a straight face. "Em here is a notorious ass-kicker in these parts. I wish you luck, my friend—you'll need it." With that, Fred turned and headed into a bar, laughing so loud he could be heard half a block away.

"That was Fred," said Em, "He's not the town drunk but sure is trying hard. I've kicked his ass many times. He likes to test me, and I'm more than willing to return the favor. Like I was taught in the academy, the police don't lose fights no matter how many cops it takes to win."

The radio kept her from continuing. "Unit 1, suspicious vehicle parked near an abandoned farm on the edge of town. Best address is 23167 Old Highway 23. The property is known to be vacant, and Mrs. Albright, who lives across the street, said she saw lights coming from inside the deserted farmhouse. I'll also notify the chief on this one."

"Unit 1, roger, en route," said Bob.

"I know this place," said Em. "It's vacant, and if Mrs. Albright—as nosey as she is—saw lights from inside, then we're sure to find someone there. So we have a burglary, at minimum."

Bob turned toward Em. "Let's stay together on this one and see what we have as we approach. Park a short distance from the farmhouse."

"Got it."

As they approached the address, Em cut the lights and hit a switch to kill the brake lights and dome light.

Getting out of their marked police vehicle, both officers were careful not to slam their doors. They spread out a few feet, with Bob leading slightly. As they neared the house, Bob pointed out a black SUV with heavily tinted windows parked near the farmhouse. He stopped to clear the SUV, but Em pressed on, anxious to kick in the door—and some ass. Bob whispered, "Clear the car first."

She stopped, hesitated, then joined him in clearing the SUV. Nothing.

Em started for the house. With years of experience in various investigations, Bob took the lead as he whispered for her to stop and get on his flank. She complied, and he moved carefully toward where the light was coming from—every step was planned, and every scan was made with tactics and safety in mind.

Em noticed his actions and did the same. She thought to herself that the dude knew his shit and that she might learn a few things from him.

As they approached the front of the house, Bob snuck a peek through a crack between two boards covering the window. He saw two men and held up two fingers to tell Em what they had. He saw no weapons and motioned to Em to take one side of the partially open door, which had been kicked in. He took the other side.

He drew his weapon. Em did the same.

After a brief pause, Bob held up three fingers. Em nodded. He counted down, and when he had one finger left, both officers rushed inside the room with their guns out.

Em yelled, "Put your hands up and don't move."

The man on the right reached for something in his jacket. Em pointed her gun at him, moving her finger off the frame and onto the trigger.

Bob took over, using a calm but firm voice. "Don't do it, buddy. Put your hands above your head and neither of you move."

The two suspects made eye contact. It appeared to Bob that the man on the right was the leader. "Do it now," he commanded again.

Slowly, both men raised their hands above their heads.

"Cover me." Bob holstered his weapon and moved behind the man on the right, carefully pulling his arms down and handcuffing him. Em moved while he was doing it so she would have a better shot if things went south.

As Bob searched the suspect, he felt a weapon. "Gun," he said as he pulled a .45-caliber semiautomatic from the man's waistband. He noted that Em was getting jumpy and was ready to shoot at the first twitch.

He quickly put suspect one on the floor. Moving to the second suspect, he saw another handgun and again announced to Em, "Gun."

"Come on, dude," exclaimed the first suspect. We just needed a place to crash for the night. We don't mean anyone harm. Just let us go, and we'll be on our way."

Em jumped on this. "Shut the fuck up, asshole, or I might sneeze and blow your brains out. Read me?"

"Fuck you, bitch."

Bob said, "Everyone quiet. You're both under arrest."

"Fuck you, too, Mr. Hotshot."

Bob proned-out both suspects. Once they were lying face down, he pointed to Em and said he would clear the house.

She nodded, keeping her gun on both suspects and hoping they would try something, anything. Her adrenaline was flowing through her body like Niagara Falls.

Bob cleared the house, and in the adjoining room, he found a large makeshift table with bags of marijuana and a set of scales on it. As Bob re-entered the room where Em had the suspects, they heard Jake yell, "Police!" as he stormed into the room with his gun drawn.

"Sorry, guys. I didn't know what might be going down." Jake holstered his weapon, as did Em and Bob. Just then, two sheriff's department cars pulled up.

When the deputies entered, the chief said, "Hi, guys. Would you mind transporting these suspects to your jail? We'll be right behind you after we tidy things up here."

The senior deputy replied, "Sure thing, Chief. Glad to help." Each deputy grabbed a suspect and loaded him up.

As the three Fairview PD officers took photos and gathered evidence, Em had a thought. "Guys, that one suspect—the loudmouth—he looked vaguely familiar. If I didn't know better, I would say he's from the Gangsters Motorcycle Club. I wonder if they're getting into the weed business. I'll follow up when we get back to the station."

"Good thinking," said Jake. "Let me know how that goes. It seems the marijuana grow business is becoming a big deal since they legalized it for medical purposes. Let's stay on this and see if we have something developing."

For Bob, the drug bust was his first action since leaving the Corps. It felt good and renewed his confidence that being a cop wasn't much different from being an MP.

As Em de-escalated, she noted how effective Bob's more methodical, disciplined approach had been. It was too

bad that they wouldn't be partners because she could learn a
lot from him.

Chapter 31 – Meet and Greet

BECAUSE JAKE HAD NO experience with marijuana-grow businesses, he did his research. He learned that as soon as Oklahoma legalized marijuana for medical purposes, there was a large influx of growers, a majority of which were illegally cashing in on forty billion—yes, with a *b*—dollars of annual marijuana profits in the state. He surmised that Green Horizon Cultivation now had a presence in Fairview and understood why they had chosen his town. Small cities like Fairview typically had inferior police departments and inadequate infrastructure, making them prime locations for additional—and illegal—activities. He wanted to learn firsthand what Green Horizon Cultivation was up to, so he headed out to their place unannounced.

As he pulled up in his outdated Dodge pickup with Fairview PD emblems on its doors, he realized there hadn't been any road or business signs. There weren't any guards along the property's road, but he did notice cameras posted intermittently along the way.

After he rounded a bend in the dirt road, Jake came upon a large Victorian home and a sizable barn. Standing outside was the lady he recognized from the night of the incident with Thomas at Rosie's. He figured her presence was either good timing on her part, or else it was because she'd been monitoring the security feeds. After parking the truck and shutting off the engine, he slid his six-foot frame out and was instantly inundated with the smell of marijuana mixed with the odor of fertilizer.

Wearing blue jeans and a plaid shirt, the lady walked briskly up to him. She immediately offered her hand while giving him a polite smile. "Nice to formally meet you, Chief Dalton. My name is Mei Zhao." Her English was perfect.

"Nice to meet you, Ms. Zhao. Our first time was rather unpleasant for you, and I apologize on behalf of the Fairview Police Department. I have since fired that officer."

"Everything happens for a purpose. I'm still learning about your culture here. Would you like to see our grow facility?" She gestured towards a stylish electric golf cart and began walking to it.

Jake joined her and took the front passenger seat. As they passed the barn, he saw Thomas exiting it. Jake said nothing but noted it as a second check mark against the supposedly legal grow.

As they drove, Mei mentioned that the city inspector had been out, hadn't found anything to cite them for, and had praised them for a professional, first-class operation.

We shall see how legit that is, thought Jake.

Arriving in front of a massive greenhouse, Jake could see through the glass that rows of marijuana plants stretched the entire length of the building. As they walked through, it all seemed to be on the up and up. Mei took her time showing him the seedling room, where tiny plants grew under delicate care, and the flowering section, where the buds would eventually be ready for harvest.

As they walked, Jake noticed numerous Chinese workers, many of whom seemed almost ghostly—quiet, focused, and not even acknowledging that either he or Mei were there. No one seemed to want to make eye contact. Jake heard snippets of their hushed conversations in their native tongue, and he caught the occasional nervous glance when they thought he wasn't watching. To Jake, the workers didn't seem to be there by choice; the sense of entrapment was unmistakable.

As Mei and Jake neared the back of the greenhouse, she led him to a dimly lit back room with a heavy wooden table at its center. She sat in a chair on one side of the table, and he sat on the other.

"Chief, I understand that an operation like this can seem...overwhelming at first glance. But let me assure you, everything we do here is above board. We've gone through all the proper channels to get the necessary licenses, and we comply with all state regulations for the cultivation and distribution of our marijuana. This facility is designed to be state-of-the-art, and we've invested heavily in the latest technology to ensure that our product is of the highest quality and meets every medical-use standard."

She gestured toward the rows of plants behind the glass wall. "I know there are rumors. There is always talk when a new operation like this starts. People speculate, and sometimes those rumors get out of hand. But I promise you, we're not involved in anything illegal. We're just trying to run a successful business like anyone else."

Jake didn't say anything when she paused, thinking it was better to let her talk and see what came out.

She smiled and tilted her head slightly before saying, "We're not so different, you and I. We're both just trying to make a living and do what's best for our people. I hope you can see that and that we can continue to work together to benefit everyone involved."

"I'm sure we can," he said, tired of the dog-and-pony show. "Thank you for the tour and your candid remarks. I'll contact you if there's any follow-up needed."

"Thank you. I'll take you back to your truck." As she drove, nothing was said, as if neither wanted to volunteer anything valuable to the other. But even though she had talked the talk, nothing she said had explained the condition of the workers, none of whom looked happy. Then, there was the matter of Thomas, who had been hired despite his actions at Rosie's. Jake didn't like any of it, and before he even started his truck, he had moved the investigation of their operation to his front burner.

WHENEVER MEI ZHAO WALKED the aisles of the illegal grow houses, she ensured the workers knew they were being closely monitored. While checking the plants and observing the workers' actions, she was especially attentive to signs of discontent or distraction and any behaviors that might suggest potential trouble.

Jie Wei was at the top of her watchlist, and his intellect and work ethic set him apart from all the others. He was becoming the go-to man when workers complained or wanted something. The trouble was, he didn't act when he heard their complaints but gave the impression that he was doing something so he could demand from them extra food rations, smokes, and money—scarce commodities for the lowly paid Chinese laborers. Mei knew his game because she'd been watching him through the facility's state-of-the-art surveillance systems.

So far, she'd let it go because it was a solid barometer of how things were going on the production side. But she talked it over with the other lieutenants of the organization, and they'd decided to change tactics with their workers. Mei had been designated as the change agent.

Walking the floor, she did her usual inspection but stopped when she reached her target. "Jie, come with me—now."

"Yes, Boss Lady."

She led him to the back of the grow facility and into a small office, where she sat down behind a desk. Standing before her, Jie clasped his hands behind his back. The room was silent except for the faint hum of climate-control machinery in the background.

"Jie, I've been hearing and seeing things. Some of the workers say you've been taking money, food, and cigarettes from them in exchange for your information and advice. Is that true?"

Jie hesitated but stayed composed. "They come to me for help. They're...grateful and offer these things as a token of appreciation. I don't ask for anything, Boss Lady."

"Grateful or desperate? There's a difference. You're in a position of influence among the workers because they see you as someone who can help them. But taking from them, even if they offer, can be...misinterpreted."

Jie nodded slowly. "I understand that, but I only take what they give willingly. I don't force anyone. And I thought they would be more focused and productive if they believed they had someone they could rely on."

Mei got the feeling he had prepared for her interview. "Focused, yes, but also indebted to you. That's a dangerous power to hold, Jie. You must understand that in this place, everything has a cost. Even your goodwill."

"I've never meant to cause trouble, Boss Lady. They trust me, and in a way, I think it keeps them from causing problems. They feel like they have someone to turn to. Many feel trapped here."

Mei leaned forward in her chair. "And that's precisely why I'm talking to you now instead of dealing with this another way. You've kept order among the workers, which is valuable to me and to this operation. But I can't have you building a power base, even if unintentionally. It complicates things and won't be tolerated."

Jie nodded his head. "I only want to help. If you think it's a problem, I'll stop. I never wanted to cause tension. I just wanted to keep things running smoothly."

Mei studied the man, trying to figure out his angle. "I believe you, Jie. But be careful. The line between helping and exploiting is thin here, and it's easy to cross without realizing it. Keep the workers in line, but don't make them obligated to you. That's not your role."

Jie bowed his head in respect. "I understand. I'll be more mindful."

Mei leaned forward and dropped her voice an octave. "Good. Because if I hear about this again, I'll have to take action. And neither of us wants that, do we?"

He looked her in the eye for a second before saying, "No, Boss Lady, we don't."

She leaned back and said in her normal tone of voice, "Okay, now get back to work, but remember, everything you do here has consequences. For you and for them. I'll be watching."

Jie turned and went back to the grow area. Mei thought he would still need close monitoring. His presence had some positives, but the negatives could affect the entire operation. Her boss in China had a lot of practice taking care of those who brought too many negatives to an enterprise. She shuddered at the thought.

THE SIGN AT THE edge of the secluded property said it all: *Trespassers Will Be Shot—Survivors Will Be Shot Again.*

The Gangsters Motorcycle Club members were always looking for new angles to bring in money. Drugs, guns, whores—they'd tried them all with mixed results. But the big bucks had remained elusive until they discovered the marijuana-grow business's humongous profits. For a year now, they've been growing and distributing weed throughout Fairview County and the surrounding area— which happened to include the town of Fairview.

The man behind Gangsters MC's newfound wealth had been Oklahoma City native Jackson "Tear Eyes" Hunter, who had tear tattoos dripping down from each eye. He was a forty-something beat-to-shit dude who had been in too many accidents and bar fights. However, Hunter had one trait that served him well—his personality, which drew people to him but put fear in his enemies. He'd grown up on the rough back streets of Oklahoma City and had gotten smarter from every encounter. Those street smarts gave him the know-how to survive and ruthlessly protect his gang's members and business interests.

When Hunter first noticed the slant-eyes from China moving into Fairview, he'd been royally pissed off and had immediately started planning how to eliminate them. Gangsters MC had been making the most money they'd ever seen, and those Chinese fucks had to go. He hadn't been sure how, but today's club meeting would provide direction and purpose.

Hunter was surrounded by his most trusted lieutenants in their secluded clubhouse bar—men who'd proven their loyalty and capability over the years. He started things off by saying, "Here's the deal. Those Chinese pricks have moved in hard and fast. They're running that grow op like they own this town. Not to mention, they're stealing some of our customers. So how do we deal with those fuckers?"

Mack "Iron" Davis, the man who always acted first at any threat, pounded his fist on the bar and said, "We hit 'em where it hurts. Burn their greenhouses to the ground. Show 'em that this is our territory and that we won't back down. Kick some ass, bro."

Snake—none of them knew his given name—who was one of the club's enforcers, fired back, saying, "We can't just torch the place without thinking it through. They've got muscle too. We go in guns blazing means we're asking for a war."

Bobby "Chains" Malone, an ex-con who'd done more time than anyone in the room, took a drag on his cigarette, then said, "War might be exactly what we need. These guys don't respect anything but strength. Remove a few of their top guys, and the rest will scatter like rats."

Hunter quickly meshed their ideas together. "We've all been around long enough to know that war means bodies on both sides. We need to be smarter than that and choke them out, piece by piece. Start with their supplies—no seeds, no grow. And look at their distribution. Take their weed and sell it to our customers."

Davis nodded. "I like that. Learn their delivery routes, intercept a few trucks, and take their weed."

"And bribe the shit out of the town's officials," said Malone. "Cops on the payroll, inspectors with a taste for cash—grease the right palms, and suddenly, the Chinese are facing fines, shutdowns, and raids. We hit 'em from every angle until they're drowning."

Hunter liked how the meeting was going. "And when they're weak enough, we take out their leaders. Quick, clean, and without drawing too much attention. They lose their head, and the rest will fall apart. It's fucking solid. Chains, find out which palms need to be greased. Iron, scope out their delivery routes. Report what you find out at our next meeting. One thing's for sure, our little sleepy hollow here will never be the same."

Chapter 34 – Mixed Emotions

THE WHOLE SAM THING was confusing to Jake. He'd gone through the motions like he was in a trance when he'd called Sam and then agreed to her visit. But ever since, he'd been asking himself what it all meant. It felt like he'd gone along with her self-invite more out of loyalty for her bravery during the bank robbery than anything else. But it seemed like she had feelings for him, and Jake had no idea why. He'd just done his job, which on that day and in that moment happened to include saving her life. If she'd chosen not to contact him, she would have only come to mind if any talk of that shooting ever came up.

The only difference from any other case was the breakfast they'd shared. He had to admit that he'd felt a rush of warmth and connection when their hands touched. But with everything that had gone down with the FID investigation and his move to Fairview, he'd forgotten about that—and her—until she'd reached out.

When Sam called a few days ago to make the final arrangements for the visit, she was surprised when Jake told her she could stay with his mother instead of at the Super 8 in town. Having her stay with him had never been an option—he wasn't that type of guy. He'd even debated about having her take an Uber from Oklahoma City, but his mom had reminded him that she'd brought up a gentleman, so he would meet Sam at the airport.

So here he was, waiting for her flight from New York City to arrive. As she finally exited the ticketed passenger area, his first thought was how beautiful she was. Perhaps, he reasoned, he was seeing her for the first time as just a regular person instead of as a hostage with a blood-splattered face.

She made eye contact with him and smiled. A sudden affection for her flowed through him, and he couldn't help but smile back.

As she walked toward him, he thought he was in one of those movies where two lovers see each other after being apart because of some faraway war. When Sam got to him, she caught him off guard as she wrapped her arms around him. Her embrace sent shivers down his spine, and he hugged her back. His mind raced with emotions he couldn't label.

Finally, he managed to say something. "Hi, Sam, nice to see you."

Shit, he thought, that was dumb.

Taking a step back, Sam said, "Jake, it's so great to see you again. I've missed you."

She was still so close to him that he could smell her fragrance. How should he answer? Had he missed her too? He'd hardly given her a thought until the past week. But he should say something similar even if it wasn't true, right?

"You look so good," she said, relieving him of the responsibility to answer. "It's like some big weight has been taken off your shoulders, like you're enjoying life in your hometown."

This time, he found some words. "Thank you, Sam. Now that you mention it, I am feeling much less stressed—it feels good. There are a lot of advantages to living life in the slow lane."

She hugged him again, surprising him a second time with the gesture. She said sheepishly, "Sorry, but you make me so happy."

He couldn't believe it when he said, "That's okay. I get it." but he didn't. Then, as if he had no control over his body, he hugged her back. He didn't say anything but kept her tightly in his arms. It just felt like the right thing to do. And he had to admit to himself that he did want to feel her close to him, which was all too confusing for the loner he was.

Eventually, Jake became more aware of the people rushing past them, and he chuckled. "I think we set up a roadblock here. How about we get your luggage?"

Sam looked around as if noticing for the first time they weren't the only people in the airport. She blushed, grabbed his hand, and led him to the baggage claim area.

BACK TO ALMOST NORMAL, Emma Parker still had nightmares about her ordeal with the now-jailed former chief Harrison, but they happened less and less. Fortunately, the newspaper's insurance paid for twice-weekly trips to Oklahoma City for therapy with a top psychiatrist.

Growing up in a family that believed seeing a shrink meant you were nuts didn't help Emma when she arrived for her first appointment, and she'd firmly believed it when she first sat down on the couch. But within minutes, her psychiatrist had her crying just by having her recount the harrowing experience she'd gone through. Emma couldn't believe she had gone from being apprehensive to releasing pent-up anger in such a short period of time. After two visits, she started to look forward to the sessions and would even talk about other things. Emma was changing back to her happy-go-lucky self again.

At the newspaper, she continued to dig up stories, and she quickly built a reputation as an honest, cut-to-the-chase, no-BS reporter. The town was quickly becoming attached to the youngster.

As an earnest reporter, Emma had her nose to the ground, sniffing out possible new stories. Although she was assigned stories every day—like a report on the Los Angeles County Natural History Museum's curator of anthropology, who had just left town—she liked coming up with fresh news that she was able to uncover. Her latest trail had led to the desk of the city building and safety inspector, Frankie Porter. She knew he'd been to the Chinese marijuana-grow property several times, but while reviewing his inspection reports, she noticed that he'd never found any code violations. That had seemed unusual to her, and she'd sensed he was holding something back. She paid him a visit.

She sat across from him at his desk and was following up on her earlier questions about how the marijuana-grow operation was going.

"Come on, Frankie, you can't tell me a huge outfit that employs dozens of workers has nothing wrong. You must have seen something."

Frankie didn't like reporters, no matter how young and cute they were. He liked being left alone, so he decided to give her the one thing that he could. "I want to be off the record on this, and you must agree."

Emma knew she was about to get somewhere and immediately replied, "Yes, off the record. What do you have for me?"

"You remember Thomas, right? That officer Dalton fired?"

She remembered how the obnoxious officer had leered at her every time she passed him. "Sure, what about him?"

"A few days ago, we ran into each other and started to BS like guys do, you know, about women. He said he had the hots—excuse me—said he liked this Chinese girl who worked at the grow. She's a lot younger than him, and I guess they have something going, but he was worried because she told him she was being forced to live there and, get this, was being forced to have sex with the big boss and his friends."

This wasn't precisely the info Emma had been looking for, but it was better than she'd imagined getting. She knew to keep her mouth shut and let him keep talking, saving her questions for when he was finished.

"The problem is"—he looked around—"Thomas loves her. He's trying to figure out how to get her off the farm. While I don't do inspections for that sort of thing, that's just not right. I feel for kids in tough situations, you know? And she has a nineteen-year-old sister trapped in that place, too."

Emma couldn't believe what she was hearing. Sex trafficking right here in Fairview, what a story. "Have you ever seen or talked to them?"

"No, but all the workers I've seen look like zombies—you know, going through the motions but with no feelings. It's like they're prisoners. Now, don't quote me on any of this, understand?"

"Yeah, no problem. I need to get going on this. We'll talk later." Emma hurried out the door and was standing in front of her boss, Charlie, a short time later.

"Judging from your behavior," he said after noticing her wide eyes and flushed cheeks, "you've got a lead on a story."

"It's big, real big. We're talking sex trafficking right here in Fairview."

"Slow down, kiddo. Take a seat and tell me everything."

She did, and after some consideration, Charlie said, "Go ahead and draft the story, but I want to talk with the chief about it so he has a heads-up."

Ten minutes later, Jake was standing in the same spot Emma had been standing, learning firsthand about the story she was writing. She was there, too, ready to answer any questions.

"First, thank you, Charlie—and you, too, Emma—for bringing this to me," said Jake. "Good work, Emma."

Jake looked back at Charlie. "How about giving me some time on this? I want to go out there, confront them, and see where it leads. My guess is nowhere, but I want to play that card and catch them off-guard. I'll get back to you with what I find out. Sound like a plan?"

Charlie took a moment to look at it from the paper's angle. "Since we have no competition on this story, which will probably go national, I can hold off for a short time. But Jake, this is too big to sit on, so you gotta keep me in the loop. Are you going out today?"

"Yep, and I'll be in touch." Jake left the newspaper office and developed a plan as he walked the short distance to the station.

Chapter 36 – The Investigation

BACK AT HIS OFFICE, Jake found Mei's business card and gave her a call. She answered on the first ring.

"Hello, Chief, how may I be of service?" Mei said in a relaxed voice.

"Hi, Mei. Something has come up that I would like to talk to you about in person today."

The line went quiet for a second. "This is such short notice. We're busy thinning and transplanting new growth, which is time-consuming." Her tone had changed as if she were on high alert. "Please give me a few days, and then we can meet. It can't be that pressing, I'm sure."

Jake didn't hesitate. "Sorry. This is an official police investigation, and it must happen today. I can either talk to you here or drive there."

Mei weighed her options and quickly came up with an answer. "Sure, I understand. I have to come to town for supplies, so what time would work for you?"

"Would 2:00 p.m. be okay?"

"Certainly, see you then."

After she hung up, Mei wondered what the big-city cop had on his mind. Had he realized the small-town chief's salary was next to nothing compared to how he was used to living in LA? He said he had to investigate something, but what? They'd bribed all the right people and had kept a tight rein on everyone at the property. Either way, everyone had their price, so she would need to be sure to take a decent amount of cash with her to the appointment.

At precisely 2:00 p.m., Mei walked into the station. Mary intercepted her because she knew power meant things to some folks, and nothing projected power like a human gatekeeper.

"Hello, I'm here to see the chief," said Mei.

"Please have a seat. I'll let him know you're here."

Mary didn't knock on Jake's door because she didn't want to seem so informal. Instead, she pressed the intercom button, and when Jake answered, she said, "Ms. Mei Zhao is here."

"Thank you, Mary. Please send her in."

Unwilling to let the woman walk into the office as if she had the authority to waltz in any time she pleased, Mary opened the door for Mei and motioned for her to enter.

When Mei entered, Jake noticed she seemed as calm and collected as ever. One chair was in front of his desk, and she took it without asking, which was fine with Jake.

Jake didn't want her to relax, so he got right to it. "Mei, I've been hearing some troubling things about what's going on at your farm. Rumors, mostly, but they're the kind that I can't just ignore."

"I'm surprised to hear that. I thought you had a good understanding of what we are doing there. Everything's legal, licensed, and above board."

He nodded. "The grow operation, sure. But what I'm hearing isn't about that. It's about the people you have working there—specifically the women. There's talk that they're not just working in the greenhouses."

"I'm sorry, but I'm not sure what you're implying. We hire a lot of workers, mostly through agencies. If there's a staff problem, I can look into it."

Jake was good at reading people and the truthfulness of their answers by paying careful attention to their eyes. In Jake's book, the eyes tell everything. Mei's eyes told him he had hit on something. He pressed her harder.

"I'm not talking about a staffing issue. I'm talking about sex trafficking. There are claims that some of the women at your farm aren't there by choice and that they're being forced into...other activities."

"I would never be involved in something like that. You're just hearing rumors, right? Does anyone have any proof?"

Jake turned up the heat even more. "That's why you're here. Before I take this further, I'm allowing you to have a chance to explain how someone might conclude that. You've been running this operation quietly and with no trouble—until now. But if these rumors are true, your grow operation will be in jeopardy."

Mei decided to take it down a notch. "You know how things are. People like to talk, especially in small towns like Fairview. Someone sees something out of the ordinary, and suddenly, there's a whole story behind it. I assure you I have nothing to hide. But if you think there's a problem, I'll cooperate fully with any investigation."

"I'm sure you understand the position I'm in. If this gets out, it's not just you who could get in trouble. My entire department could be dragged into this mess, especially if it looks like we've been turning a blind eye."

Mei quickly contemplated the money in her purse but didn't want to play that hand yet. She was getting mixed signals about him.

"I get it. But I hope you also understand that accusations like these could destroy everything I've built. I have nothing to gain from this kind of trouble, and I want to keep things clean just as much as you do."

Jake knew he needed to keep the pressure on. "I want to believe that. But you need to know that we'll be watching. And if something doesn't add up, it won't be just a friendly chat next time."

Their eyes locked.

"I appreciate the warning. But you won't find anything illegal at the farm. We're running a legitimate business, and I'll make sure to address any concerns with the workers immediately."

As Mei left the office, she knew she needed to move quickly.

And Jake knew he did too.

AS THE WEEKS PASSED after Sam's visit with Jake, she made some life-altering decisions. None had been easy, but all had been made with Jake in the loop and considered their budding relationship, something entirely new for both. Sam had realized that after the traumas of the bank robbery and of being taken hostage, she valued being closer to Jake for his emotional support. Surviving such an event also allowed her to re-evaluate her priorities in life. Moving to Oklahoma would be a way to have a fresh start and to leave behind her lingering fears about what had happened. To her, Jake's companionship and protection would nourish her soul so she could move on. Besides, she had strong feelings for him.

With the two in agreement, Sam rented a U-Haul, used a small crew to load her things, and said goodbye to LA. Throughout the whole process, she'd done it without a second of doubt and without any qualms about being with Jake. The nightmares had gone, and life was looking better.

After arriving in Fairview, they decided not to rush things, so Jake helped Sam move in with his mom. He couldn't tell who was happier about the decision, his mom or Sam. Agnes had been excited to have someone to share her time with and to talk about the latest book she was reading. It worked out for Jake too, as things had been picking up rapidly at work and he didn't have time for idle chats or deep relationship conversations because he was focused on Green Horizon Cultivation.

Chapter 38 – Harvest

LI CHENG HAD CALLED for everyone to be on deck for the first significant harvest of the show crop and the illicit crop. He walked the aisles, a .45 strapped prominently on his hip to discourage any disturbances by the fifty workers. His lieutenants followed along with him: Zhi Hao, his second-in-command; Bin Wang; Mei Zhao; and Jun Zhou, who had been putting the finishing touches on the operation's distribution plan.

The air throughout the grow facilities was thick with the pungent aroma of cannabis—rows of mature marijuana plants, most over six feet tall, filled every inch of space. The workers moved methodically through the plants, trimming and cutting them with specialized electric tools.

Mei closely watched Jie Wei. Even after their little heart-to-heart, she still suspected he encouraged disobedience by the workers so they could obtain better living and working conditions. She would eliminate him if she ever caught him in the act. To help her with that, she'd ordered Yong Chen, her most trusted worker, to report any irregular activities.

But Jie was a crafty man. He made plans to escape the drudgery and repression of working in the grow. He would be nobody's slave, putting in ten to twelve hours a day for subpar rations and little pay. He had an idea.

Knowing he was continually watched, Jie had gone about his business, working harder than usual and not saying one word to anyone. But in secret, Jie had befriended a young worker, Ling, who usually worked in one of the drying rooms. He had promised Ling that if he helped carry through with the plan, he could come with him when he escaped.

Unlike the workers, who didn't have a shift change, the guards regularly changed shifts at the legal and illegal grow areas. As the guards were preoccupied with changeover activities, Ling located his hidden matches and bottle of gasoline. Quickly, he poured the bottle's contents all over the back of the drying room. With a flick of his wrist, he lit a match, dropped it onto the accelerant, and calmly exited the building and headed toward the community bathroom. As Ling was doing his part, Jie asked his supervisor for permission to take a piss, and he also headed to the bathroom.

Moments later, the entire complex went on fire alert as billowing black smoke poured out the windows of the illegal grow house and towered into the sky. The drying room was set up with fire suppression sprinklers, but the intense heat was too much for the system. Security units responded with a water truck to extinguish the growing fire.

During their planned commotion, which occupied the focus of the entire staff, Jie and Ling walked away from the complex. Although they tripped the border alarms, security didn't see the alerts because all of their attention was on fighting the fire.

Passersby on the old highway saw smoke and jammed 911 lines with calls. The Fairview Fire Department called for their volunteer firefighters to report to the station. Word of the fire quickly spread to city hall. When Jake heard about it from the dispatcher, he jumped in his police vehicle to go investigate.

While fighting the fire, Li realized the nosey country folk who owned neighboring lands had most likely called the authorities. He ordered some of his security personnel to go to the property's entrance and turn everyone away. They were not to accept any help. Li couldn't afford to have anyone discover the illegal grow area.

In a small community like Fairview, it didn't take much to get the curious to hop in their cars and drive out to see what was happening. When they turned down the unmarked access road, they didn't see fire trucks; instead, two large trucks formed a barricade so no one could get past. Standing next to the trucks were four tough-looking Chinese men with heavy jackets on. One of the men kept making a circular motion with his hand, telling everyone to turn around. They did, but in doing so, the lookie-loos caused a traffic jam on the highway.

Jie and his accomplice made it off the property, where they got the attention of a Mexican rancher stuck in traffic. It appeared that the rancher wasn't there for the show but wanted to keep going. He didn't speak Chinese but understood that the men needed a ride. He motioned for them to get in the back of his truck and, seeing a break in traffic, passed everyone in line. It never occurred to him to ask the two men anything because he'd been in their position many times when white people questioned his every move—he resented that sort of treatment and didn't want to subject others to it.

When the two Fairview FD fire trucks arrived, they got caught up in the traffic jam and, even with sirens blasting, got nowhere. Finally, the captain ordered the trucks to go off-road around the traffic. Not only did they bypass the curious, but they also went around the roadblock. The guards, who couldn't stop the large trucks, promptly notified Li.

As this happened, Jake arrived, and, catching a glimpse of the off-roading fire department, followed the trucks through the brush. As the first responders drove down the property's access road, Mei stopped them at the Victorian mansion. Standing beside her was an armed, mean-looking dude who, by his demeanor, made it clear no one was going any further.

The law in Oklahoma, and in most rural communities across the nation, states that even if a fire is on private property and the owner says to leave, the fire department and law enforcement officials have the authority to enter. The law, rooted in the idea that what happens on one property can affect others in the community, puts society's rights over the rights of the property owner. The fire captain explained it to the two Chinese standing in their way, but he couldn't get anywhere with them.

Jake walked up to the group and, without any introduction, told Mei and her guard to move aside or he would arrest them for interfering with an official police matter. He then told the fire chief to go ahead and extinguish the fire. Mei and Zhi looked at each other and then reluctantly moved aside.

Following the plume of smoke, Jake and the fire trucks found a road off the beaten track that took them toward the fire. As they passed building after building, Jake noticed how different they were from the glass-enclosed greenhouses he'd been shown. These buildings had solid walls, and the only windows were high up, which prevented anyone from easily seeing what was inside.

When they arrived at the burning building, they saw several armed Chinese men attempting to extinguish the fire. The captain of the Fairview FD waved them off and had his firefighters lay out their hoses to fight the diminishing fire, which was now just dark black smoke that smelled like marijuana. He ordered all his men to put on their breathing apparatuses.

Jake stood upwind. Mei approached him without her guard. "The talk among our workers is that someone sneaked a smoke and somehow started this blaze. We thought we could put it out ourselves without troubling anyone."

"So why did you have guards blocking the only entrance, and why did you try to stop the fire department back by the house? Seems to me you wanted to keep this part of your business hidden from public view."

"We thought a volunteer fire department meant everyone in town came to extinguish a fire. It's obvious to us now that only those who are trained respond. We didn't want the whole town's populace on the property—you never know who could get hurt, and then we would be liable for damages. But then, a lot of unauthorized people did show up, didn't they?"

Jake couldn't wholly discount her explanation, and he remained silent to see if she would fill in the quiet space.

The tactic worked because she added, "Security in our business is paramount. We have nothing to hide, but I understand your concern. The plants grew faster than anticipated, and we needed more room to ensure the main buildings weren't overcrowded, so we built additional structures to space out the plants and maximize their yield. We simply did what any farmer would have done. It's all above board—just an operational necessity."

Jake looked around the area, taking in the numerous buildings he thought had been purposefully hidden. "Thank you, Mei. I'll be in touch. And since I'm here and authorized I will see if the firefighters need more help." He walked to the fire captain.

"Sorry to interrupt, Bruce, but could you do me a favor? See if you can determine what happened here. I'm not sure I buy her story that a worker accidentally started the fire by smoking."

"Sure thing, Chief."

"And could you put on a show about not needing my help right now?" Jake winked, and Bruce heartily complied.

Chapter 39 – Dark Secret

EMMA THOUGHT IT WAS time for her article on sex trafficking to be published, so Charlie contacted Jake. After thanking the paper for holding off on publishing the article, Jake gave them the green light. He knew the story would change the opinion of the citizens of Fairview toward the marijuana-grow operation and its owners. When he got the edition, he read the story.

Hidden in Plain Sight: A Grow Farm's Dark Secret
By Emma Parker, staff reporter

Fairview, a town known for its quiet streets and close-knit community, has long prided itself on being a safe place to live and raise a family. But behind the facade of rural tranquility, a dark and horrifying secret has taken root—a secret that threatens to tear the very fabric of our town apart.

For months, rumors have swirled around a particular grow operation on the outskirts of Fairview. Officially, it is a licensed facility cultivating marijuana for medical purposes. Unofficially, it has become the epicenter of a much more sinister enterprise: sex trafficking.

According to an anonymous source, a citizen with deep ties to our community, young Chinese women have been brought to this facility under false pretenses. Promised work and a new life in America, they instead found themselves trapped in a nightmare, forced into sexual servitude by those who control the grow operation of Green Horizon Cultivation LLC.

One girl, whom we'll call "Ling" was lured from her home in China with the promise of a good job and a new beginning. Instead, she was stripped of her identity, isolated from the outside world, and forced to serve the "clients" who frequent the farm. Ling and other girls like her are held under constant watch, their every move controlled, their cries for help unheard by the outside world.

The Fairview citizen recounted how a man who works at the farm fell in love with Ling. His feelings for her grew as he realized the true nature of her captivity, and he wanted this story published to bring attention to this illegal activity. "It's not just about one girl," he told me. "It's about all of them. They're scared, alone, and they need someone to speak up for them."

His story, if true, paints a harrowing picture of what lies behind the guarded gates of this grow operation. But without official recognition or legal action, the truth remains buried, and the girls remain imprisoned.

This article is not an accusation but a call to action. The allegations of sex trafficking on this grow farm demand a thorough and transparent investigation by local and state authorities. Fairview deserves to know the truth, and these young women deserve a chance at the freedom they were promised.

As a community, we cannot turn a blind eye to what may be happening right under our noses. The time to act is now, before more lives are destroyed and more futures are stolen.

For those who know something, no matter how small, I urge you to come forward. Together, we can bring an end to this nightmare and restore the safety and dignity of our town.

Editor's note: This piece is based on anonymous sources and unverified claims. The Fairview Gazette is committed to investigative journalism and will continue to follow this story as it develops.

Chapter 41 – The Press Conference

MEI CHATTED WITH THE three people beside her while the independent video crew set up their equipment. They were providing a feed to networks that were reporting on the allegation that the Chinese marijuana farm was involved in sex trafficking.

Sitting with Mei were the two sisters, Fen and Qiu Huang, one of whom was referred to as Ling in the Fairview Gazette's article. Next to them was Thomas. After the director gave Mei the "action" sign, Mei got up from her seat and approached a podium that had a prominent sign reading:

Green Horizon Cultivation LLC

Helping Those in Need

"Good morning," said Mei, "thank you for taking the time to hear our response to some serious allegations made in yesterday's article in the *Fairview Gazette*. I'm Mei Zhao, and I oversee operations at Green Horizon Cultivation LLC's Fairview grow farm. The claims of sex trafficking and exploitation at our site are not only false but also deeply damaging to the integrity of our business and our community."

She paused to let the weight of her words settle. Keeping her attention on the camera, she continued, "I want to introduce you to Fen and Qiu." She gestured to the two seated young women. They stood and joined her. The sisters looked nervous, held hands, and nodded slightly to the cameras.

Mei lightly patted the shoulder of the sister closest to her. "These are the women who were mentioned in the article. As you can see, they are here of their own free will and have a statement they would like to make." Stepping back, Mei gently guided the sisters to the podium.

Fen looked at the microphone and glanced at the interpreter standing off-camera to her right. In a quivering voice, Fen said, "The things in the article are not true. We came here to work, and we are treated well." The interpreter repeated her statement in English.

Gaining strength from her words, Fen continued, "We are not prisoners and have never been forced to do anything against our will."

As the translator interpreted her words, Qiu nodded and added, "We don't know why this story was made up, but it's hurtful and wrong. We want everyone to know that we are safe and that what was published is a lie."

While the interpreter relayed the last statement, Mei nodded encouragingly as the sisters stepped back and returned to their seats. Mei turned her attention to Thomas, who shifted uneasily in his chair. He was the linchpin of Emma's article—the former Fairview cop who had supposedly exposed the truth. Now, he looked more like a man caught in his own personal hell than like a whistleblower.

Thomas stepped to the podium, visibly uncomfortable under the gaze of the cameras. He took a deep breath, then said, "Look, I made some mistakes"—his voice cracked a bit—"and I...I said things I shouldn't have. There's no trafficking. I was angry, and I made up the whole story." He glanced quickly at Qiu, but she stared straight ahead. "The truth is, I was involved with one of these women, and when things didn't work out between us, I said things out of spite. I never meant for any of this to happen. I'm very sorry."

Mei gently touched Thomas's shoulder and guided him toward his chair. She then faced the camera again, her expression a mixture of empathy and resolve.

"It's clear that personal issues have been taken out of context and blown into something far from the truth," Mei stated. "We understand that emotions can lead to poor decisions, but we also know the damage that false accusations can cause—to our business, to our community, and most importantly, to innocent people like Fen and Qiu."

Mei paused to dab a handkerchief at her eyes. As she spoke again, her voice was firm. "Our grow operation has always adhered to the highest standards of legality and respect for human rights. We have nothing to hide and will fully cooperate with any official inquiries. But let's be clear. These accusations were based on a personal vendetta, not facts. We ask the public to see this for what it was—a misunderstanding fueled by hurt feelings and rejected love, not criminal activity. Thank you." As Mei turned back to the girls, the camera light went out.

Mei had flipped the story, and now it was up to the public to decide who they believed: the determined rookie journalist who was perhaps trying to make a name for herself, or the composed businesswoman who refuted it all with the calm conviction of a true professional. As the camera crew packed up their equipment, Mei silently congratulated herself.

Chapter 42 – Transport

LI CHENG, THE SON of one of the most powerful crime lords in China, was attempting to tap into the vast profits available from the marijuana-grow business in the US, specifically in Oklahoma. But his father was upset with him. Reports that the cops were investigating his operation for sex trafficking, that a fire had exposed the illegal grow houses to local authorities, and that two of the grow's Chinese workers had escaped all highlighted the need for change. As the first shipments of the illegal marijuana were being prepared for transportation, Li was finally ready to deliver some good news to his father. Tonight's shipment would bring in enough money to expand the operation, to pay off officials, and to secure their foothold in the region.

Three nondescript semi-trailers packed full of vacuum-sealed packages of marijuana were ready for the road. Each truck had a driver and an armed guard, all chosen for their loyalty. In one truck was Yong Chen, who was once again promoted, this time to lead guard. He advanced because the boss man had noted his devotion to the Cheng family and, most importantly, his ability to be trusted—all essential attributes demanded by Li. Yong had even picked up some English.

As Yong sat in the truck, his eyes were already scanning the darkness. The trucks would leave at midnight and travel separately to three metropolitan cities. Li's lieutenant in charge of distribution, Jun Zhou had laid out all three routes, each to avoid the major highways that had higher law enforcement presence, CCTV surveillance, random checkpoints, and an increased likelihood of being stopped for a routine safety inspection. By traveling secondary highways and back roads, they would appear to be just another truck passing through.

At 3:00 a.m., Yong's 600-horsepower 18-wheeler was traveling east on Oklahoma State Route 60 with a Laughing Buddha bobblehead on the dashboard bouncing in rhythm with the uneven pavement. Yong was alert and looking for anything unusual, which wasn't much at that time of the morning. His .45 occasionally bumped against his hip, a feeling he was still getting used to.

As they rounded a long, sweeping turn, a large pickup truck suddenly pulled from between two small hills. It stopped on the desolate two-lane highway, completely blocking it. Two hooded men jumped out of the pickup. Yong's driver slammed on the brakes, causing the entire rig to shudder under the sudden strain. The tires screamed for traction against the asphalt—a deafening combination of burning rubber, grinding gears, and the guttural howl of the engine. As the truck ground to a halt, the large trailer swung slightly, teetering on the edge of control before settling back behind the cab with a *thump*.

Everything fell eerily silent except for the hiss of the air brakes. The driver's hands trembled noticeably on the wheel as he slowly exhaled, the weight of near disaster settling in. Just feet ahead, the pickup sat motionless.

Yong glanced in the mirror and saw another large pickup block them in from behind, its black finish illuminated by the semi's emergency lights. They were trapped. Yong went for his weapon. But just as he did so, masked individuals emerged from the brush, all heavily armed and wearing black balaclava hoodies. His hand froze on the grips.

Yong whispered to his driver, "Don't do anything. We are heavily outnumbered." Yong pulled his hand away from his gun.

A large man approached Yong's side of the truck. Yong immediately noticed the man's balaclava failed to conceal tattoos that looked like tears in the corners of his eyes. The man tapped the barrel of his weapon on Yong's window and yelled, "Get out of the truck, nice and slow."

Yong carefully opened the door and stepped out, making sure to keep his hands visible. The driver followed suit. Both men were directed to the front of the truck, where the headlights made them look like dual silhouettes. They were face to face with a dozen or so armed men who had encircled them, all with their weapons pointed at them.

Tear Eyes looked Yong up and down, sizing him up as a minimal threat. "You're carrying something that belongs to us now," he said, gesturing to the trailer behind them with his gun. "We'll be taking your ride...that is if you don't mind?"

Yong said with a heavy accent, "No English."

"Fucking Chinese bastards," uttered Tear Eyes. "Check them for weapons, then tie them to that tree over there." Once again swinging his 6-inch .44 magnum like a conductor's baton, he pointed to a tree twenty feet off the highway.

Four men stepped forward, grabbed the two Chinese men, and forced them over to the tree after taking Yong's .45. The burly Americans tied the two around the tree using cord cuffs and finished the job by putting black tape over their mouths.

At Tear Eyes' signal, two of his men climbed into the semi's cab. The truck's engine rumbled to life again, and the

Gangsters Motorcycle Club driver slowly backed into a pasture entrance to turn around. Within minutes, the rest of the gang disappeared, and the bobblehead in the semi began to bounce again from the uneven pavement of Route 60. The truck was now traveling west toward Van Buren County with new owners.

Chapter 42 – Warning

WALKING AROUND HIS LUXURIOUS villa tucked away in a gated community in Shenzhen, China, with more security than even the president of China had, Ming Cheng was pissed. An angry Dragon Head wasn't a good thing for the people who worked for him, including some of the meanest, most notorious gang members in the People's Republic of China. Those setting up his communications for a meeting with his son had been given five minutes to make everything work. None of them wanted to be a second late.

The comms specialists used the same encrypted video conferencing software hosted on the Chinese military's private servers. The software included self-destructing messages, encrypted file sharing, and no data logging. In other words, it was rock-solid and perfect for Ming's discussion of his syndicate's operation in Oklahoma.

At exactly 8:00 a.m., Ming sat down behind his heavily carved walnut desk and waited for the comms specialist to bring up a video image of Li and his lieutenants on Ming's computer screen. It was early evening in Fairview, so nobody there would have an excuse not to be present.

Ming's screen lit up, showing a high-ceilinged, dark-paneled room and five people sitting at a large meeting table. Everyone from the Oklahoma crew stood and bowed.

"You all make me sick," Ming said before they could sit back down. "Do any of you understand the gravity of what has happened? I send you to Oklahoma to establish a profitable operation, and instead, I hear of escaped workers, whores, a fire that destroyed part of our harvest, and an entire truckload of our product taken by some street thugs."

"Father"—the camera zoomed to a headshot of a very nervous-looking son—"we underestimated the Gangsters Motorcycle Club. They've been a constant nuisance, but we didn't expect them to be bold enough to hijack—"

"Underestimated? Is that the excuse you bring to me? I gave you everything you needed to succeed—money, manpower, influence—and you repay me with failure after failure."

"Boss Man," the camera efficiently zoomed to Zhi Hao, "the fire was an unforeseen act of sabotage. We believe some of the workers were plotting behind our backs, but we're tightening security now, and—"

"Unforeseen? Everything is unforeseen until it happens. Number one, Lieutenant, it's your job to see it coming. If you can't control a few laborers, how do you expect to manage an entire operation?"

Li responded, "We will deal with the traitors, Father. We've also increased security, doubled the guards, and conducted thorough interrogations to root out any more who might be plotting against us. The situation is under control."

Ming leaned forward. "Do you think this looks under control to me, Li? You're sitting there, half a world away, while I must answer to our investors. They don't care about your excuses. They only care about results."

Zhi Hao said, "Boss Man, we've already started planning a counterattack against the Gangsters Motorcycle Club. We'll hit them hard, take back what's ours, and send a message that—"

"A counterattack?" screamed Ming. "You want to start a war over this and risk bringing even more heat down on our operation? If you'd done your job correctly in the first place, we wouldn't be in this mess."

"Please give us a little more time, Father," Li said. "We can fix this. We'll take care of the Gangsters quietly, strengthen our hold on the operation, and ensure nothing like this happens again."

"Time? Do you think I'm in the business of giving second chances? You think I can afford to let you bungle this operation and hope that somehow, you'll miraculously turn things around?"

The room in Oklahoma was silent, the echo of the Dragon Head's words haunting everyone who stood there. They all knew their lives would depend on what Ming decided next. Li bowed his head. The others followed his lead and bowed theirs, too.

Ming remembered when he'd stood before his own father with his head bowed, so ashamed of being a failure that he would have welcomed a death sentence. He'd learned a hard lesson in that moment of humility.

"Li, you will eliminate the Gangsters, but you will do it quietly so that no one can trace it to us. You will find the escapees and those responsible for the fire and make them suffer so that no one else thinks of crossing us again. Understand?"

"Yes, Father," Li said, his head still bowed. "I won't fail you."

"You know what will happen if you do," said Ming, his voice dripping with menace. He sat back and nodded to the comms specialist, and the screen went black. Like it had been up to Ming years ago to prove his ability to overcome setbacks, it was Li's turn now.

In Oklahoma, Li raised his head after a few seconds of silence, verifying that the screen was black. He looked around the table at his lieutenants, who had also lifted their heads and were now staring at him. It was clear that they all knew failure was not an option because, this time, the consequences would be fatal to them all. Such was life in the syndicate.

SAM WAS HAVING DOUBTS about living in Fairview, having no job and seemingly no profession. While Jake had been busy being the police chief, she'd been withering with no real direction. And she realized that balancing the long-term effects of her trauma with her need for independence was a battle. Although grateful for Jake's support, she wanted to prove to him that she could again stand on her own two feet. She decided to get her name out there to other Oklahoma anthropologists.

Sam also noticed that Jake was spending more and more time at the office. He talked a lot about the politics in Fairview and his new role in it. He was adjusting, but she could tell that he didn't like it. To Sam, it was simple. She wanted more out of life than being a stay-at-home girlfriend; it was time to fix that.

Chapter 44 – Payback

Fairview, usually half asleep due to perennial small-town boredom, snapped out of it after hearing a rumor that the Gangsters Motorcycle Club had hijacked the Chinese grow farm's first marijuana shipment. Despite all the chatter, Tear Eyes Hunter and the other Gangster members had kept quiet. Such a bold move didn't need to be sullied with bragging.

On the other hand, the Dragon Head's message had been loud and clear to the five members of his syndicate who ran the Chinese grow farm. Zhi Hao had spent a few days working up a plan. Little did the grow house workers know, a storm brewed underneath the usual serious expression of one of their overseers. The hijack had been the worst humiliation in Zhi's career and couldn't go unanswered. They'd lost product, profit, and respectability.

Workers near Zhi noticed a slight change in his expression when he pulled out his phone, punched in a number, and spoke briefly and firmly in Mandarin before hanging up. They worried when he smiled after setting his plan in motion.

As the Dragon Head had ordered, Zhi's plan had centered on action with businesslike acumen. He had used his network of informants and Chinese syndicate resources to gather information on the Gangsters MC. He'd also surveilled them to learn about their routines, weaknesses, and personal habits. It hadn't taken long before Zhi had pinpointed key members and their favorite hangouts—a run-down bar on the outskirts of town. In this dilapidated clubhouse, they kept their stolen goods and a garage they used as a front for their illicit operations.

Applying pressure in small ways, Zhi disrupted their drug deals, intercepted shipments, and spread rumors that sowed distrust within the club. As tensions rose among the gang members and paranoia set in, they struggled to figure out who was sabotaging them.

Zhi's methodical approach was psychological warfare, meant to weaken targets before delivering the final blow. The Gangsters MC, once a tight-knit unit, had started to fray under the stress. Tear Eyes had become frustrated and increasingly unstable, and he'd started to make poor decisions that only compounded their problems.

After weeks of undermining the club's operations, Zhi was ready to strike. He'd arranged an ambush at the gang's clubhouse, where he'd heard they planned to celebrate their recent success and their move into big-time distribution.

The night was moonless, and the sky was overcast and heavy with the promise of rain. Dressed in black tactical gear, wearing hoods and latex gloves, and armed with silenced weapons, Zhi and his men moved through the shadows like ghosts. They quietly approached the clubhouse; their movements choreographed and deliberate to avoid the occasional beam of light from the lone guard's flashlight.

Inside the clubhouse, the Gangsters were in the midst of a rowdy celebration. Along with the sound of clinking glasses and booming laughter, music blared from an old stereo in the corner of the run-down former bar. Tear Eyes sat at the head of a long table and entertained his crew with stories of their most significant score—the hijacking of the Chinese weed shipment.

Zhi gave a hand signal, and his team moved into position. Yong Chen fired one shot from his silenced .45 to eliminate the guard. Two other men opened the front door and threw several flash bangs inside, which exploded with blinding light and deafening noise.

The inside of the clubhouse plunged into pandemonium. Bikers stumbled around, disoriented, clutching their ears and rubbing their eyes. No one responded when the Chinese enforcers breached the unguarded entrance.

As the initial shock of the raid left the Gangsters reeling, Zhi's men moved through the room. The room quickly filled with the shouts of panicked gang members trying to regroup. Some attempted to fight back, overturning tables for cover and firing blindly into the smoke-filled room, but their resistance was disorganized and futile against the disciplined Chinese killers.

Tear Eyes, caught in the center of the melee, tried desperately to rally his crew, but it didn't go well. He grabbed his shotgun from beneath a table and headed to a storage room.

Zhi noticed that the gang's leader hurried into a second room. He quickly followed him, smashing through the door. There was a loud explosion as Tear Eyes fired his sawed-off 12-gauge at Zhi, who had already dived to the floor. The buckshot whizzed over his head, blowing the door from its hinges. Zhi returned fire, striking Tear Eyes in the left shoulder and spinning him around.

Tear Eyes dropped his shotgun as he hit the floor. Recovering quickly, he grabbed the shotgun and brought it up to fire. But Zhi had anticipated his move and quickly kicked it from his grasp. When Tear Eyes looked up, he saw a .45 pointed at his head.

Tear Eyes scooted backward, pressed himself against the wall as leverage, and struggled to his feet. Bleeding heavily from his shoulder, he said, "Come on, man, we can work something out—I'll make sure you get your weed back."

Zhi locked eyes with him. "Too late for that, asshole." He pulled the trigger, sending a bullet straight into Tear Eyes' forehead and splattering brains all over himself and the wall. Zhi stepped back as the man shed his last tear and crumpled to the floor.

When Zhi re-entered the main room, he stepped over two dead Gangsters as he surveyed the results of his raid. He ordered his men to secure the area, load the two wounded bikers into one of their trucks, and then immediately set in motion Zhi's cover-up plan to place the blame on Mike Carson, who ran a much smaller illegal marijuana grow in the area but, like all growers, had visions of enlarging his share of the market.

Two of Zhi's workers had recently infiltrated Carson's operation, explaining that they were dissatisfied with the pay and working conditions at the Chinese grow. Once inside the much smaller operation, they had carefully removed some tools, careful not to contaminate those tools with their own fingerprints. They also had acquired a label with Carson's logo on it. Zhi had duplicated those labels and, using the LLC's weed, had packaged up a load to make it appear that the bikers had stolen it from Carson's operation.

Zhi now planted the tools and the Carson-labeled weed in the Gangster's clubhouse where the police would find them. He also left behind some clothing from the Carson grow, courtesy of his two infiltrators. While he did all that, the rest of his men scoured the area and retrieved all of their brass casings.

When the Chinese men finally got into their two trucks, Zhi called in a second team. They brought a water truck to wet down the dirt area where the assault team had parked, and they left the property with the water spraying behind them, effectively erasing all tire marks. The water crew didn't have to spray around the building because Zhi had thought of having the assaulters wear disposable shoe coverings so no boot impressions would be left behind.

After returning to their own property, Zhi had his men take the two wounded bikers to an enclosed room in the back of one of the illegal grow houses. Sitting the two prisoners in chairs next to each other, they handcuffed them and tied them to their chairs as Zhi approached the first gang member.

Looking back and forth between each man, Zhi nodded to his interpreter, who stood behind them. He didn't really need an interpreter, but using one projected power and gave him an advantage. Pausing every so often, he said, "I will only give you one chance at this, so I suggest you listen carefully and make the right decision. I want each of you to agree to forget all about us and, when we let you go, to tell the police that Carson's group attacked your clubhouse over a hijacking you made on one of his distribution trucks."

The large biker on the right, with blood still oozing out of his right shoulder and left leg, tried to get up. "Fuck you, you slant-eyed pricks." He spit into Zhi's face.

Zhi drew his .45 so fast he even surprised himself. He promptly shot the man in the head, spraying blood over everyone, including the man's friend sitting next to him. The echo from the gunshot was deafening, as was the thud of the bullet penetrating the man's skull.

Turning to the remaining biker, Zhi noticed the man had wet himself. "What do you have to say, my friend? Do you care to go along with my suggestion?"

The bearded biker with tattoos covering every part of his exposed skin didn't hesitate. "Come on, man, I'm married with two kids. I hang out with these guys for fun, not for running drugs and getting into shootouts."

Zhi put the barrel of his still-hot gun against the man's tattooed forehead. "Just yes or no will do." He pushed his gun with more force, causing the man's head to tilt back so he was looking straight up at Zhi and his .45 with crossed eyes. "Last chance."

"Don't shoot, man. I'll do whatever you ask."

Zhi lowered his weapon slightly, and the biker's head came back to level. "Thank you for sharing your family situation so that we know who to kill besides you if you fuck this up."

"Dude, none of this shit is worth it. I just want to get back to my family. I'll actually enjoy burning these dumb assholes for their stupidity." With that, the man wept. Zhi explained how things would work, then had the biker dumped near the clubhouse. Now they would wait to see just how well a police department of five could investigate the shooting.

Chapter 45 – Smooth Operations

AFTER A ROUGH START, Jun Zhou had gotten the distribution operation going again. In an off-limits room in the Victorian mansion, he had a large map of Oklahoma and, next to it, a map of the US. Both were filled with colorful pins, each detailing a successful delivery. Mei Zhao was with him because she wanted to see where the product went and to discuss logistics and deception. Jun was very good at both, and today, she would see exactly how good.

Jun called Yong Chen, whom he had stationed at a small garage on the outskirts of Fairview. The garage was nondescript, and nobody paid any attention to it. It was just a place with no substance.

"Yong, you ready?" he asked.

Yong was now involved with all important aspects of the business. He looked over the garage's interior and the fleet of vans, each one a different make and model. The place smelled of gasoline, oil, and rubber, a cover for the actual business of the garage.

"All set," Yong said and glanced at the clock on the wall. "The drivers are in place. The first truck of the day should be there shortly," he said in an even, almost mechanical, voice.

Yong trusted his men implicitly. They knew the risks, but they also knew the rewards. Most of his drivers were experienced truckers who were down on their luck and needed a fresh cash infusion. The big plus was that they didn't ask questions. They also knew how to navigate the roads without drawing attention and would understand how to handle long hauls and deal with potential checkpoints or weigh stations.

Ten minutes later, a faded blue Ford with a plumbing company logo prominently displayed on the side arrived at the garage. The van was from a small-time business George had purchased and would be used only for running dope and laundering money.

On the security screens in the Victorian mansion's off-limits room, Jun and Mei watched the van's driver, a young man in his twenties with a baseball cap on backward, as he backed into the garage's covered loading bay. Two workers swiftly moved crates of tightly packed marijuana into the van and covered them with genuine plumbing supplies. Yong supervised the process to ensure the weight distribution was perfect to avoid suspicion during a potential stop. After he nodded to the driver, the van took off onto the quiet back roads that led out of Fairview.

Mei watched all the blips on a different monitor, each representing a GPS tracker on a different van. They moved like clockwork, carefully coordinated and never overlapping or on the same routes. Mei sipped her coffee and couldn't help but admire Jun's carefully planned routine. Each van headed to a different city and different distributors, all part of the web he had woven across the state and beyond.

As the last van drove off, Yong followed it in his black SUV, keeping a distance but always within sight of the next checkpoint—in this case, a small diner off Route 412 where drivers would swap vehicles. The operation was designed to minimize risk; no driver would know the entire route or the final destination. They were just cogs in the machine, moving pieces in the great puzzle of the Chinese syndicate's distribution network.

In Tulsa, one of the vans pulled into a warehouse owned by a shell company that George had set up. The regional distributor, a burly man with a thick beard and piercing eyes, oversaw the unloading. He checked the weight and quality before giving a thumbs-up to his crew. They would handle the next stage, breaking the bulk into smaller packages for street-level dealers. The system was seamless, and the handoffs were clean and precise.

At the grow operation, Mei watched the last van's GPS blip arrive in Tulsa. She exhaled a breath she didn't realize she had been holding while watching that last van's final miles. The cycle would start again tomorrow, but for now, the five Fairview operators of the Cheng Syndicate had earned another day.

Chapter 46 – New Leadership

THE ELEVEN GANGSTERS MC members who hadn't attended the celebration entered their clubhouse, or what was left of it. The raucous partying the Gangsters MC lived by had been replaced by death and destruction. One of the dead was Tear Eyes, who'd fought against the attackers but had taken a round to the head. As two grizzled old-time bikers paced the floor, staring at the bodies and blood, it seemed to those present that no one had a plan to get out of this mess. One man held a half-opened package of weed with a Carson label on it. Another man kicked at a piece of fabric on the floor, a shirt with the Carson logo. Everyone else was wandering around the room aimlessly.

All except one man, Tyler Granger, who happened to be the club's newest full-patch member—a man known more for kicking ass than for making speeches.

"Alright, listen up," the clean-shaven thirty-year-old hollered, "This ain't the time for feeling sorry. We've got a fucking mess to clean up, and we're not gonna let this shit bring the cops down on us. Rocco—get our fallen brothers into the back of the van. We'll take care of that problem shortly. The rest of you start clearing the tables and chairs. Everything that's broken goes out back. We're torching it all, no traces left behind. Mitch, you and Doc scrub the floor using bleach, ammonia, or whatever it takes. I don't want a damn stain left when we're done."

The older guys hesitated initially; their pride stung by taking orders from the youngest full member. But Ty's cold glance told them he was taking charge. Always a man who led by example, Ty got a bucket of water and was on his hands and knees scrubbing the blood off the floor.

As the men worked, Ty stopped momentarily to survey the room. To him, this was more than just cleaning up a crime scene—this was about restoring order and showing that the Gangsters MC wouldn't roll over and die. Ty could feel the weight of the patch on his back, the responsibility pressing down on him, but it wasn't fear that gripped him. It was something sharper, more dangerous. It was a need for vengeance.

As the crew was getting on top of things, Ty gathered them around him. He held up the Carson shirt. "This mess isn't just about us losing our president and our brothers. It's a declaration of war. We all know it wasn't Carson who did this"—he tossed the shirt back down on the floor—"because they're small-time. It was the fucking Chinese because we took their weed. I was there. My initiation was to drive the truck once we took it away from them." He looked at the bikers who'd sponsored him, and they nodded to confirm what Ty said. "Can we let them think they can muscle in on our turf, screw with our business, kill our brothers, and walk away? Hell no. We're gonna strike back but in a smart way. And we're not gonna leave them a chance to retaliate."

The bikers grunted their approval, so Ty continued, "We start by hitting their supply lines, disrupting their grow ops, and scaring off their buyers. We make them bleed money until they've got nothing left but bad debts and empty promises. And when they're on their knees begging for mercy—that's when we crush them. Not just a warning but a full-on reckoning."

As he talked confidently about his plan, he could see more members nodding in agreement. Most were not much into leading but would follow the right man into battle. Ty was that man.

By the time the sun rose, the clubhouse was back in order, but it wasn't just the clean floors; the club's purpose was restored, and everyone's focus was sharper than ever. The men once lost in a fog of anger and confusion, now looked to Ty respectfully and were ready to follow his lead.

Ty scanned the room again, looking somber. "We can't leave anything to chance—no bodies, no funerals, no graves. We're not giving the cops or the Chinese any leverage. We do this right, and we walk away clean. We mess it up, and we're looking at a whole different set of problems."

He went over how they would transport the bodies to a seldom-used maintenance shop owned by one of the Gangsters. The next part wasn't pleasant as he explained how he and one more volunteer would dismember the bodies with tools from the shop. It would be gruesome work, but it was a necessary evil to make the disposal easier and prevent identification.

To destroy the remains, Ty suggested using industrial-grade acid—something the club had used before to dispose of smaller, organic evidence. They would put the body parts in barrels filled with the corrosive liquid, allowing them to break down over time. The acid would dissolve the flesh, bones, and clothing, leaving nothing but sludge that could be disposed of without a trace.

After the bodies were dissolved and disposed of, the Gangsters would thoroughly clean the shop, scrubbing every surface, burning any clothes or tools used in the process, and taking special care to destroy any traces of blood or DNA. The barrels and other equipment would be thoroughly cleaned and filled with oil or gasoline. They would tell the families that the brothers had to skip town and stay on the run or risk getting sent to the state pen.

Ty reminded everyone of the stakes. "We do this smart and honor our brothers by keeping the club strong. We mess up, and we're not just dealing with cops—we're giving the Chinese exactly what they want. So double-check everything, trust no one outside this room, and remember that the club comes first."

As they all left the now-clean clubhouse, Ty was more than ready to exact revenge on the Chinese who had dared to strike at the heart of his club.

CHIEF JAKE DALTON HAD been handling the phone because Mary was out of the office. The calls were about the usual stuff, like the family cat stuck in a tree, noisy neighbors, the occasional theft, and so on. Most people calling had no idea they were talking with the chief.

As he was working on the deployment schedule for the next month, he answered another call. "Listen," said the caller, "I won't say this twice. There was a shooting at the Gangster's clubhouse, and Tear Eyes is dead. The Chinese did it." After a click, there was nothing but a dial tone.

Jake straightened, his senses suddenly on alert. He stared at the phone, feeling the familiar tingling of suspicion make his old burns itch. This wasn't the first time he'd gotten an anonymous tip. They were usually dead ends, but every now and then, something stuck.

After giving it another moment, he noted the call on his desk calendar, which was already full of small notes. He thought the call was legit since he'd heard rumblings of a feud between the two groups. But how could there have been no reports, not even any calls? It seemed like every unusual sound in and around Fairview was reported.

He got up from his desk, thinking it was time to visit those asshole Gangsters. Even though he had checked his 9mm Glock when he'd gotten dressed—like he did every morning—he did another press check to ensure a round was in the chamber. He stopped by his radio operator and told her he was heading out to visit the Gangsters at their clubhouse. He asked her to have his one on-duty unit head that way as a backup.

The clubhouse was just outside the city limits, near an abandoned farm. Fortunately, the PD and the Sheriff's Department agreed that under "special circumstances" they could conduct investigations in each other's jurisdictions. Jake considered this one of those cases because it involved the Chinese who operated in his jurisdiction.

Pulling up to the site, Jake cut the engine and stepped out onto what should have been dry, dusty dirt. Instead, it was a little damp, putting a layer of mud on his boots. That was unusual as there had been no rain for a month. The location was remote, a perfect spot for something to go down—no immediate neighbors with prying eyes and no passing cars.

The sun was beginning to dip, casting an orange glow over everything. Jake adjusted his Sam Browne duty belt and scanned the surroundings. He spotted the run-down building that passed for a clubhouse. It was tucked behind a row of scrubby trees and a rusted chain-link fence that did little to hide the place's true nature. A few motorcycles were parked haphazardly out front, their chrome glinting in the fading light. It was quiet.

Jake took a slow walk around the perimeter, scanning every inch of the lot. The place looked recently cleaned, and that was off. It was too pristine for a gang's hangout. He stopped near one side of the building. Faint traces of old, dried stains clung stubbornly to the ground, almost imperceptible unless you knew where and what to look for.

Crouching down, he ran his fingers over the dirt. The stain could've been anything, but the clean-up had been hasty, which made him suspicious. He stood up and continued his visual inspection, making mental notes of the inconsistencies: a slightly off-color patch on the wall that looked recently painted and a trash bin that smelled strongly of bleach.

He glanced at the side of the wood structure, where the telltale signs of bullet holes were poorly concealed beneath a coat of fresh paint. Every little detail fed his growing suspicion that something significant had happened here.

He heard a noise and spun around. The clubhouse door creaked open, and a biker emerged, flying his colors and walking toward Jake with a noticeable swagger, a half-smirk, half-scowl plastered on his face. The guy was big and clean-shaven, with the kind of presence that demanded your attention. Jake was ready to go for his Glock at the first sign of trouble.

"Chief Dalton," the man grunted and halted several feet away. "You lost, or just sightseeing?"

Jake kept his expression neutral. "Howdy. And who might you be?"

"Just your average biker having a beer with some friends. But call me Ty, like all my friends do," he said, then flashed a smart-assed grin.

Jake looked him over, scanning for weapons. He didn't see any. "I got a tip and figured I should come check it out. You know anything about a shooting here a few days back?"

Ty shrugged. "No shootings here, Chief. We're just a bunch of law-abiding citizens enjoying the peace and quiet of the countryside. You know how it is." His grin widened, but his eyes stayed focused on Jake.

Both heard an approaching car and turned in that direction. Jake noted it was Bob Spectrum, his newest hire. He and Ty watched as the older officer carefully approached, standing a little behind the chief and to the side.

"Hey there, son," Ty said. "Glad you could make it. Why don't you join us? We were just talking about us law-abiding bikers."

Bob nodded and stood his ground, carefully checking the area for anything that might be a threat.

Jake wasn't buying Ty's act. "The place looks like it's had a bit of work done. Fresh paint, a couple of repairs, just routine maintenance, I suppose?"

Ty's smile faltered just a fraction. "We like to keep the place tidy. Can't have the neighbors complaining, right?"

Jake said nothing, his gaze still wandering over the scene. He knew Ty was lying, but without hard evidence, all he had was a hunch. Still, he thought, hunches were often the breadcrumbs that led to something bigger. "Right. Well, I'll be sure to keep an eye on things. Wouldn't want any trouble spilling over into town."

Ty crossed his arms. "Don't worry. If there was trouble, you'd be the first to know."

Jake locked eyes with Ty. "I'm sure I would." Turning to his backup, he said, "Thanks, Bob," then headed to his truck. He watched Bob slowly return to his squad car, never fully taking his eyes off Ty and the building. Jake made a mental note to mention how good his officer's safety tactics were. Not bad for a small-town cop, he thought.

Once in his truck, Jake figured he would dig deeper, keep the pressure on, and wait for someone to slip up. Because, as he knew all too well, secrets had a way of surfacing, and he had a knack for finding them.

WITH JAKE BUSY AS chief and Sam living with his mom, their budding relationship had not gone far. To keep things fresh, every Friday night was date night. Both had committed to a no-excuses policy for their special night. But this Friday, instead of the usual dinner at Rosie's, they'd decided to drive to Oklahoma City for the weekend. Sam had some important news to share, and she suggested the trip, which Jake quickly agreed to. Besides, he thought, the trip would be a fun drive in his Porsche—a chance to stretch its legs a little.

Heading south down State Route 74 for their hour-and-a-half drive, Jake blasted *Alt Nation* on his radio, listening to a newer group he had just discovered: Maneskin, an Italian rock group that seemed to hit all the right notes for him.

While he was enjoying them, Sam made it clear she would much rather listen to jazz, the only music Jake could not get into. So they settled on dividing the drive time between *Alt Nation* and *Real Jazz*. They loved their tunes, so the time passed quickly as each tried to appreciate the other's taste. It worked perfectly, except when Jake passed slower traffic on the two-lane highway, which was quite often. Jake turned the music down for every pass to hear his Porsche kick in as he gunned it. To Jake, that was real music. As for

Sam, she was just happy to see him content, which wasn't all that often because of the stress of his work. She patted him on his leg after each pass. They were having fun.

Sam had had plenty of free time since resigning from the museum. She'd meticulously planned the entire weekend as if it were their honeymoon—a bold move, especially since they hadn't slept together yet. Both knew that was about to change, and the thought filled them with quiet excitement, bringing frequent smiles that warmed them from the inside out.

Pulling up to their digs in Oklahoma City, the stylish Fordson Hotel—formerly the 21C Museum Hotel—they saw the plaque stating the place was listed on the Historic Hotels of America register. They thought it was so cool that the 1916 building used to be a Ford Model T assembly plant.

Jake enjoyed every aspect as he parked out front. First, it was how his lava-orange Porsche harmonized with the reddish brick of the hotel. He took several pictures of his car, with only one of Sam in it. He loved how people gawked as he unloaded their luggage from the car's front and back trunks. "Where's the engine?" said one passerby. People weren't used to car engines not being in either the front or rear of the car. Most had never heard of mid-engines.

As the two entered the lobby, they took turns taking each other's picture underneath the upside-down stuffed white polar bear. When they entered their suite with its huge wraparound windows, they stopped to marvel at the enormous king-size bed, blushing like teenagers because they knew they would be in it together later that night. It was all so exciting.

With some time before dinner, the two took a leisurely boat ride along the Bricktown Canal to soak in the city's historical and modern architecture. They found the perfect seat on the boat and held hands during their sightseeing voyage. It was an ideal afternoon full of laughter, flirting, and, above all else, simply enjoying each other's company.

To cap off the day, they went to Vast, a rooftop restaurant at the Devon Tower, offering the city's most panoramic view. In no hurry to order dinner, the two enjoyed a glass of fine California cabernet sauvignon as the sun set. It was time, Sam thought.

"So you know I've put out feelers around Oklahoma in anthropology, but I'm not finding anything that interests me."

Jake nodded, waiting to see where the conversation was going. Is she heading back to LA? he wondered. The thought wasn't pleasant.

"This past Monday," she continued, "I got a call from the Fairview Chamber of Commerce. Are you ready for this?" She took a sip of her wine. "They asked me to be their next president."

Jake set his wine down and grabbed Sam's hand. "That's exciting, the Fairview Chamber of Commerce— wow. That's so cool. I sure didn't see that coming."

"Neither did I, but I guess if you have the credentials in small towns, they come looking for you. They told me in the interview on Thursday that they loved my resume, especially since I was the head of the museum's anthropology department in LA. They envisioned me putting Fairview on the map for its numerous archaeological sites that reflect the state's rich Native American history and prehistoric cultures. How cool is that?"

"Sam, that's awesome. I'm so happy for you—and for us. I've hated seeing your intellect wasted here in Fairview. Now I see a sparkle in your eyes again. I love it."

Sam gripped his hand even tighter. "That means so much. Your support is everything to me." She laughed and said, "It's a good thing you agree because I start in two weeks."

"Even better, because I can't wait to see you in your new digs. Speaking of which, I think we should consider a new home for you, something closer to town, like my place." He held a hand, continuing, "Please don't say anything yet. We can talk about it more this weekend."

"Wow, you're a fast mover all of a sudden."

"I guess I'm finally coming out of my shell and seeing my world with you in it. Anyway, let's talk about it later. Excuse the pun, but it's a big move for both of us."

"Okay, I agree. And excuse *my* pun," she said, smiling, "but we can sleep on it."

"Then let's order dinner before we start thinking of bedtime." Sam blushed, and Jake winked at her.

Returning to their beautiful, expansive room, the two took some time to take in the artwork on the walls, with the city's lights shining softly through the large windows. They shared a glass of bourbon while laughing over recent memories. When they finally embraced, any remnants of thoughts about what had brought them together melted away.

As the night deepened, so did their connection. Their barriers fell away, leaving them with nothing but the quiet certainty of the moment. The morning light found them tangled in the sheets, the evidence of their newfound intimacy marked by the comfortable closeness that hadn't been fully there before. They didn't need to speak about it; the easy smiles and warmth between them said enough.

The rest of the weekend in Oklahoma City flew by in a blur of laughter and special moments. They wandered through the Oklahoma City Museum of Art, where Sam teased Jake about his lack of appreciation for abstract art. Jake feigned interest as she explained things, but he enjoyed watching her light up with every new exhibit. They strolled along the Bricktown Canal, stopping for coffee and having conversations that felt lighter than they had in the past.

As they drove home, the setting sun painted the sky in hues that matched their mood—warm and bright, as if promising something more. Sam glanced over at Jake, a contented smile on her lips. He reached over and squeezed her hand, and they both knew they were heading back more than just happy—they were heading back closer than they had ever been. They decided to make Jake's home theirs as a final tribute to their fun weekend.

Chapter 49 – Rosie's

Li Cheng sat in the leather chair behind his massive mahogany desk, which was the focal point of his large office. This was the heart of all his operations. Li conducted his most important meetings here at the rear of the large Victorian house, past the living areas and behind a sliding, carved wooden door. The office was a striking blend of Victorian elegance, modern efficiency, and subtle nods to his Chinese heritage. The walls were lined with tall, built-in bookshelves filled with leather-bound books, some genuinely antique and others reproductions hollowed out to hide ledgers and cash. Several small jade statues and porcelain vases were on display, adding a touch of elegance. A large antique globe sat in the corner next to a small bar cart stocked with expensive liquor and traditional Chinese *baijiu*, so he could offer drinks to select guests.

In front of the desk were two smaller, equally luxurious leather chairs for visitors, and a small, low table was between them. A Chinese folding screen, painted with an elaborate dragon motif, stood to one side of the room, partially hiding a small alcove where a safe was discreetly built into the wall and accessible only by a biometric lock.

Six strategically placed straight-back chairs surrounded Li's desk, all neatly facing him. As his father had taught him, it was necessary to continually make it clear who was the leader and who wasn't. This setup worked perfectly.

His lieutenants, along with George Sullivan, occupied five of the chairs. Today's meeting was another important one. Li had been reflecting on the millions of dollars coming in from the sale of his illegal marijuana and on how to launder the truckloads of money so the feds wouldn't catch on. He was now dumping large piles of cash into shell companies, smurfing, real estate investments, cryptocurrency, and offshore accounts. However, one of the easiest and safest methods was to funnel it through cash businesses. By using those businesses, his accountant could inflate sales numbers, reporting higher monthly totals than what occurred, and then deposit illegal cash as part of the "earnings." His accountant could also create fake invoices and receipts for services or goods never provided or sold, forming a paper trail substantiating the extra cash as legitimate business revenue. But Li needed to acquire those cash businesses, so he got the meeting going.

"The numbers don't lie," said Li. "We're pulling in more cash than our current businesses can handle. If we don't expand our laundering operation, we'll drown in dirty money."

Zhi Hao quickly replied: "We already own half the block downtown. We've got laundromats, a convenience store, and our maintenance store. I could see to it that we push a bit more cash through those places."

"That's not enough. We need something more versatile, something steady and cash-heavy that won't raise suspicion."

George Sullivan stood out as the only non-Asian in the meeting. But his value to the operation was immense. He was not only their frontman but a man with insider knowledge of the town. "Boss Man," he said respectfully, proving he was catching on to their jargon, "I respectfully suggest Rosie's restaurant. It's family owned and has lots of cash transactions. After some research, and bribing certain people, I know the owner is having trouble making payroll and needs cash for equipment and repairs to the building."

Mei jumped at that. "The restaurant's a family legacy. Why would she sell? Besides, Rosie's is well-known in the community. People will notice if there's a sudden change in operations, especially with new Asian owners. If we're too aggressive, it'll draw unwanted attention."

Zhi said, "We could keep her on as the face of the business for a while, making it look like nothing changed. Meanwhile, we could funnel the money through the restaurant, ramp up the cash flow with fake sales, and clean up our books."

George flashed a wide grin. "Exactly. It's low-profile, already trusted by the community, and perfectly set up for growth. With a bit of renovation, we could double its capacity and turn it into the go-to place, not just in this county but for folks living in surrounding counties as well. Cash could flow through and vanish into thin air."

"And what if she refuses?" said Mei. "We can't afford delays or her suspicion. This needs to go through now."

"Listen," Zhi said, leaning forward, "We can make it so she won't have a choice. We present a generous offer—firm but enticing—and if she resists, we apply the pressure. Trust me. I can make this happen if we're on the same page."

Everyone agreed, and Li said, "We should move quickly. The longer we wait, the more exposed we are. Let's finalize the numbers and contact the owner. Keep it clean, but make it clear—we don't take no for an answer."

Mei quickly volunteered. "I know enough to approach her, and I should be able to wrap this up within a week, Boss Man."

Standing up, Li said, "Good. We need this to work. Too much is riding on it. I don't want a single bill left dirty, understood?"

Everyone nodded, and the meeting ended with the murmur of chairs sliding back and footsteps echoing in the otherwise silent room. Mei lingered momentarily, staring at the financial projections that Li had displayed on a screen. She knew this was just another step in the game, a necessary move to keep their operation thriving and ahead of any law enforcement or federal scrutiny.

Chapter 50 – A Plan

THE FAIRVIEW POLICE DEPARTMENT patrolled a town upward of two thousand souls and had just four officers and the chief to do the job. At least once a week, everyone on the force was present at the morning shift change, and today, Jake had an idea he wanted to run by the troops.

After taking a sip from his second cup of coffee, he said, "As we've already discussed, this marijuana-grow business is changing the way our community functions. The Gangsters Motorcycle Club, and especially the Chinese owners of the grow farm, are the two main contributors to the change. We have fires and prostitution allegations at the Chinese grow plus a rumored hijacking of product by the Gangsters, which I believe has escalated into gang warfare."

Jake paused for another sip. Noting everyone nodding their agreement, he continued, "There's also a possible illegal grow on the Chinese farm of such enormous proportions that, if not stopped, could make Fairview a suburb of Beijing. In other words, Green Horizon Cultivation's Chinese owners could own this town and control everything in it. We need to be proactive."

"Proactive how?" said Em Carter. "We can't even keep up with the petty bullshit that always happens in this town. Sorry, Chief, but I don't see what we can do."

Two officers nodded in agreement, but not Bob Spectrum, the only one with years of experience.

"Slow down, Em." Jake downed the rest of his coffee. "I haven't finished yet. With limited resources, we must be creative. I've read about aerial drones used by the Ukrainian armed forces and by some of the larger metropolitan PDs in the US. Maybe we need a drone to fly over Green Horizon's legal grow, and in the process, we might see what's really up."

Jake let that sink in, but it didn't appear everyone thought it was a good idea. Then Bob spoke up.

"In the Corps, we had an extensive surveillance operation, and I saw firsthand how valuable these drones can be. It's a game-changer if we can get our hands on one."

"Thanks, Bob, for sharing that." Turning his attention to the others, Jake laid out the plan. "I'll get us a drone and a pilot, but in the meantime, I want each of you to pay special attention when any of our Chinese friends come to town. Find some probable cause to stop them, talk with them, and see if you can get some intel. Contact me with anything you find, and I'll let you know what I turn up."

Chapter 51 – The Offer

IT WAS FIVE MINUTES before closing, and Nancy was clearing off the last booth in Rosie's, slowly wiping the counter with precise strokes as she considered her life. She was only thirty-five, but today she felt much older. It was hard working tables ten hours a day while running the place and raising a child, just like her mother had done. But the restaurant was her mom's legacy, one Nancy would never part with, no matter how much anyone offered. She owed that to her mom.

Outside, the old neon sign flashed *osie's* because the *R* had burned out two years ago. She'd tried to get people from Oklahoma City to fix it, but no one worked on old neon lights anymore. Her last order of business each night was to turn the sign off, so she headed to the front entrance.

Just then, the door swung open. Mei Zhao entered, dressed sharply in a tailored black suit and with her dark hair slicked back in a tight ponytail. Alongside her was a big man dressed in a loose-fitting black suit. He drew one side of his jacket away from his body, and Nancy saw that he had a gun.

She said, "We're closing now. You'll have to come back tomorrow."

"I'm not here for dinner," Mei said. "I'm here to talk business."

"I already told your people I'm not selling."

Mei glanced around the empty restaurant, taking in the worn booths and faded wallpaper. She stepped in farther, her heels clicking against the tiled floor. She leaned casually against the counter, just inches away from Nancy. "This place has potential, far more than you're letting it have. You could have a new menu and maybe even some live music with a little investment. This could be the hottest spot in town, even in all the surrounding counties. It could make you very wealthy."

Nancy backed up a step and stared at Mei. Her fingers tightened around the damp cloth in her hand as if it were Mei's neck. She'd heard all this BS many times, but there was no way she was going to give up the restaurant—it would be like burying her mom all over again.

"You're wasting your time, Ms. Zhao. Like I've said before, I'm not interested."

Mei pursed her lips, then made eye contact with her bodyguard. He reached inside his jacket and wrapped his hand around the grips of his weapon.

Nancy thought, Shit, is the asshole going to shoot me?

"Now that I have your attention , I don't think you understand the opportunity here. We're offering you more than this place is worth and a chance to retire comfortably. You've been working your ass off for years, right? Don't you want a well-deserved break?"

"What I deserve is to keep what's mine. This place was my mother's. It's not for sale."

Mei got in her face. She was so close that Nancy could smell her perfume—some expensive stuff, no doubt. In a voice like a growl but came out in a whisper, Mei said, "I admire your loyalty. But to be clear"—pounding her finger right into Nancy's chest—"Refusing me isn't an option anymore."

Nancy felt her heartbeat pick up speed but was determined she wouldn't let this tiny bitch control her or her business. She wanted the woman out of her place for good. She stepped forward until the toes of her shoes nearly scuffed Mei's high heels. Looking as tough as she could, she said, "I don't care what you say. I'm not selling my soul for a paycheck. Do you think you can waltz in here and bully me out of my place? That's not gonna happen. Now get the fuck out of my store."

Mei didn't seem moved by Nancy's bravado. Staring Nancy down, she slowly pulled her phone from her pocket, tapped the screen once, and flipped it around so it was inches from Nancy's face.

Nancy had to back up a little so her eyes could focus on the screen. What she saw turned her face ghostly white. On the screen was a photo of her son, Timmy, walking home from school.

"Timmy, isn't it?" said Mei in a calm, almost friendly tone. "Cute kid. It would be a shame if something happened to him because his mother made the wrong decision."

Nancy stumbled back. She couldn't believe it. They'd spied on her only child. There was no telling what these bastards would do to him.

Mei slowly slid the phone back into her pocket, never taking her eyes off Nancy.

Her voice shaking, Nancy said, "You stay away from him. You hear me?"

"Or what, are you going to beat me up?" Mei smiled. "Think clearly now. I'm done playing games with you. You know what you need to do, and we'll make it all official. You just need to sign some papers. You get a huge payout, Timmy stays safe, and we get what we want. Everyone wins."

For a moment, Nancy tried to figure out how to keep Timmy safe if she refused again. But there was no way she could guarantee it. They had the resources to find and follow him no matter where she sent him.

Nancy slumped as the fight drained from her body. "Fine. I'll sign. But you never come after my family again, you hear me?"

Mei snapped her fingers, and her bodyguard produced a folded stack of papers from a pocket inside his jacket. Mei took them, unfolded them, and laid them on the countertop. The man roughly slammed a pen on top of the papers.

Nancy reluctantly picked up the pen with a shaky hand. Not wanting to give Mei any more satisfaction, she held back tears as she signed her name to the papers in the stack. When she was done, she threw the pen onto the counter.

Mei said, "You have one week to get any personal items out of here." Without another word, she took the documents, spun around, and left, her bodyguard glancing back with a smug look.

After the door closed behind them, Nancy sat in a booth and looked around the empty restaurant. This was where she had grown up, where she had felt her mother's presence after she had died. It had always been a place of warmth, but now she felt cold, as if her mom had just died again, knowing that her daughter had handed her legacy over to a wolf in a tailored suit.

JAKE STOOD ON THE sprawling farm that bordered the land housing the Chinese grow operation. The sun had just dipped below the horizon, casting long shadows across the fields. Beside him, Agent Lila Hayes from the Oklahoma Bureau of Narcotics was preparing a drone for its flight over the Chinese grow farm. Jake felt Lila was young, confident, and knowledgeable about her job. He'd been told she was the go-to person for drone surveillance missions. She used the agency's new Enterprise Matrice drone for flight.

"You sure this thing can get us what we need?" Jake asked. To Jake, the sleek black machine looked like something out of a sci-fi movie. The LAPD had often used helicopters and fixed-wing aircraft, as they could use altitude to stay out of sight, but Jake had never encountered drones.

"If there's something to see, we'll see it," Lila said. "This dude is equipped with 20-megapixel resolution and thermal imaging. And since it can fly silent, it's like a ghost with eyes."

Jake appreciated her confidence. He knew the illegal grow operation was big, but just how big was the question. He'd had reports of night shifts, unusual power consumption, and many trucks coming and going, but still no solid proof of the operation's scale.

Lila finished the preflight checks and launched the drone into the darkening sky. It rose steadily, becoming a barely discernible speck. The two watched the feed on her tablet as the drone ascended and swept over the farm's perimeter before flying a preprogrammed grid.

The first report arrived quickly. Sounding excited, she said, "Look at that." She tilted the tablet to give Jake a better view.

The high-resolution camera showed row after row of greenhouses, the glass glowing faintly from powerful grow lights. Jake could see movement—workers darting between structures, carts loaded with supplies, and the distinct presence of armed guards patrolling the grounds. The sheer number of greenhouses was staggering. Jake counted six, then eight, then lost track as Lila continued a slow, methodical sweep.

"They've got at least twelve full-size greenhouses separate from the legal grow area," Lila reported, zooming in to capture more detail. "Each one could easily hold hundreds of plants. They're running a serious operation here."

Jake watched as the drone's camera panned over some large generators, their exhaust hidden by cleverly designed venting systems. Lila swung the drone around to capture the large barn's main processing area. Just visible were some drying racks and a trimming station.

Shaking his head, Jake said, "This isn't just a grow, it's a damn factory. They're processing everything on-site."

"Looks like they've got the whole supply chain," said Lila. "Growing, processing, packing, and shipping, all in one place."

Jake noticed some trucks coming and going at the top of the monitor. "Take a look at the vehicle traffic," he said while pointing at the activity.

Lila shifted the drone's focus to the vehicles using a back entrance that was partially hidden from the main road. Jake noted the mix of trucks and vans, some of which he recognized from previous surveillance.

After the drone made one more pass over the substantial operation, Jake said he had seen enough. The size and complexity meant they were dealing with more than just a grow—it was an empire. Lila expertly maneuvered the drone back to its starting point and landed it softly on the grassy field.

During their debrief, Lila said, "We'll compile the footage and start building a case. This is more than enough to get the ball rolling. You were right to bring us in."

"Thanks for coming out, and nice work. This changes everything from my point of view. Now I know what we have."

As she left, Jake felt a mix of satisfaction and unease. He had the proof he needed, but the situation was far more dangerous than he had previously thought. The Chinese grow operation was not just a local problem but a full-scale criminal enterprise. Countering it would require all the resources they could muster and much more. He knew the Chinese would not go down easily, not with that much money invested.

Chapter 53 – Payoff

Frankie Porter was living the high life. With regular payoffs from the Chinese to turn a blind eye to their illegal activity, the city inspector's bank account was thriving. He had treated himself to a new truck, had made every repair his house needed, and had splurged on new clothes and gifts for his wife and son. Life couldn't have been better. The inspections were a breeze since the grow operation maintained high standards. He chose not to dig too deep and conveniently overlooked greenhouses that, on paper, didn't even exist. Frankie felt no guilt; he did his job and earned generous "tips" from Mei.

One Friday after work, he decided he deserved a beer for all his hard work. While he was sitting at the Black Stallion bar, a clean-cut guy approached him and introduced himself as Ty Granger, the president of a local motorcycle club.

Ty bought Frankie a beer and told him he had a proposition that would make Frankie some good money. Frankie thought the offer would have to be pretty good because he was flush.

"What do you have in mind, Ty?" Frankie asked as the bartender set a third beer in front of him.

With Merle Haggard's *Mama Tried* blasting away in the background from an ageless jukebox, Ty took a sip from his longneck beer. "As I understand, you do the city inspections at the Chinese farm, right?"

Frankie paused, trying to figure out where this was going. "Yeah, that's one of the places I inspect. Why?"

"Well, my friend, if I pay you $50,000 now, perhaps during your next inspection, you'll find some glaring violations within their operation. And if one of those violations shuts them down for, say a month, then there's another $50,000 available to you. After that, who knows? A hardworking man like yourself deserves to be compensated."

Frankie almost choked as he was taking a swig of his beer. Holy shit, he thought, that's a lot of money.

But Frankie was a quick thinker and immediately had a plan to milk both income sources. "Well, I'm always thorough, but perhaps not thorough enough. Just recently, I thought there was room for improvement when I was examining the Chinese operation." He took a long pull from his beer. "Tell you what, they're probably due for a surprise inspection next week. You take care of your end before then, and I'll try my best to do mine, if you get my drift."

Ty smiled broadly. "Tell you what, I think you should check your work mailbox on Monday for a special delivery."

As the jukebox loaded another song, *Whiskey Bent and Hell Bound* by Hank Williams Jr., the two men ordered another beer and talked like best friends—with mutual interests.

Chapter 54 – Home Sweet Home

As Sam was nearing Jake's home, using Agnes's pickup truck to haul her belongings, she hoped she was making the right decision. The move from LA was stressful enough. Going from a bustling city of four million to a town of two thousand was definitely a culture shock. But now, moving in with Jake made Sam feel like she was saying yes to a marriage proposal. She could hear his calm voice saying they could try this out together and see if it worked, which reassured her. And if it didn't work...well, she wouldn't let her mind go down that road.

Sam made the final turn down his driveway. Jake's modest two-bedroom home sat on a quiet street on the outskirts of Fairview. It was surrounded by tall oaks that provided shade and a sense of privacy.

She got out of the truck, pulled out a bulging box, and scanned the house with a mix of anticipation and trepidation. The house was cozy, a far cry from her sleek LA apartment, but it felt more like a home—a place where she could finally breathe. She loved the big backyard and fire pit, where they had already spent many pleasant evenings together.

Jake came running out to meet her, with a big smile on his face. "Welcome home," he said, taking the box of anthropology books from her. Sam smiled back, feeling a surge of warmth at his words. It was the first time she felt she had a place to call home since moving to Fairview.

As they approached the front door, Jake suddenly set the books down and picked her up in his arms. "Sorry, I just think it's proper that you enter as my partner if we're going to live here together. It's the only way I've pictured this moment." After gently kissing her forehead, he pushed the door open with his foot, and in they went.

As Jake gently set her down, Sam felt like she had just floated back to earth. After she landed, she grabbed Jake, jumped up and wrapped her legs around him, and gave him a long, passionate kiss. "That's my thank-you, sir, for the grand entrance that this woman did not see coming. What a fabulous beginning."

Getting to work unloading the truck, they worked together to unpack Sam's things and find places for them amid Jake's sparse decor—if he even had such a thing. Jake watched Sam carefully remove her favorite abstract painting and hang it above the mantel. It was the first splash of bright color in the room for who knew how long.

Jake bit his lip when Sam wasn't looking. "That looks good there," he said. He knew there had to be some give and take in any relationship, and the painting was tough for a guy who wasn't into art, let alone abstract art.

"Come on, Jake, tell me the truth—you don't think it clashes?"

"With what?" They both smiled at that one.

The days that followed were a mixture of settling in and navigating the new dynamics of living together. Sam was meticulous and liked things in their place, a habit she picked up from years of living in an apartment where space was at a premium. On the other hand, Jake was more laid-back, leaving his boots by the door and his jacket draped over the back of a chair.

They had their minor squabbles—Sam's insistence on a no-shoes-inside policy and Jake's mixing whites and darks in the washing machine—but they laughed them off more often than not. They were learning each other's habits and finding a balance between their differences.

Despite the minor quirks and adjustments, there was an undeniable ease to their living arrangement. They found comfort in the little routines they built together—sharing morning coffee on the porch, taking evening walks, and spending quiet nights next to each other on the couch, either watching documentaries or reading.

To celebrate Sam's move, Jake suggested they host a small dinner for some of the people who had become their circle in Fairview. Sam was initially hesitant; she wasn't sure how she felt about publicly sharing this new chapter of her life. But Jake assured her it would be casual—just a few friends, good food, and a chance to unwind.

On the night of the dinner, Sam was a bundle of nerves as she prepared her favorite dish from her LA days—an elaborate vegetarian lasagna. Knowing his friends would want more, Jake grilled steaks outside, a nod to their guests' simpler meat-and-potatoes preferences.

As the evening unfolded, the house filled with laughter and the clinking of glasses. Mary, the chief's secretary, made a toast to the new couple. During the toast, Sam watched Jake from across the room. He was in his element—cracking jokes, making sure everyone had a drink, and stealing glances at her with a look that made her feel all warm inside. Sam realized just how much she had come to care for him and how much this place, town, and man had become a part of her.

After the last guest left and the house was quiet, Sam and Jake settled on the couch, exhausted but content. Sam leaned into Jake and rested her head on his shoulder.

"Tonight was nice," she said softly.

"Yeah, it was." Jake wrapped his arm around her. They sat in comfortable silence for a while, basking in the afterglow of the evening. Then he added, "I'm glad you're here, Sam. Really glad."

Sam looked up at him, her eyes bright. "Me too. It feels...right."

Jake leaned down and kissed her gently. It wasn't a grand gesture, just a simple, quiet moment that spoke volumes. They were building something real, something that felt like it could last. The former LA cop and the former hostage both felt at peace for the first time in a long time.

Chapter 55 – Expanding the Operation

ORDERS HAD COME DOWN to Li Cheng from his father, who wanted more even though he appreciated the growth operation's positive turnaround. The Cheng Syndicate was moving to the top tier in China, which meant additional income was needed to make payroll and increase wealth. Cheng Ming had a lucrative sex trafficking operation in China and reasoned the US operation could make more.

Ming told his son he would send several more girls to bolster Li's stable, but he would leave it up to Li to get at least one American girl to augment client offerings. Ming also authorized Li to use some of the profits from the grow operation to buy a house in Fairview as a brothel.

Li went to work immediately by contacting George. He explained that the house had to look like any other property in Fairview—modest, well-maintained, and unassuming. The home needed to be situated in a less conspicuous neighborhood, like on the outskirts of town. Additionally, similar-looking homes had to surround it, and it needed to be close enough to the main roads for easy access.

George found the perfect home in one day and closed the cash deal two weeks later after paying the seller a nice under-the-table thank-you bribe. All the paperwork was in his name, keeping any link to the Chinese anonymous.

George also oversaw the installation of the security system for the house. He put up security cameras around the perimeter, covering all entry points and providing a clear view of the street. To avoid suspicion from neighbors, he camouflaged the cameras. A high wooden fence was erected to enclose the backyard, providing privacy and making it difficult for outsiders to see. He also installed keypad access terminals at all entrances.

Following specific orders from Li, George divided the oversized bedrooms into smaller ones explicitly designed for the business. He also built additional small bedrooms in the basement of the house. George installed electronic keypads on each door, operated from the outside, and left the door unlocked when a customer was inside. The rooms had minimal furniture: a bed, a vanity dresser, and one small chair. There was a community bathroom at the end of the hall. The windows were heavily tinted, and each room had hidden cameras to monitor the girls so they couldn't entice a customer to help them escape. The only thing left was filling each room with a worker.

Chapter 56 – Wrong Choices

Seventeen-year-old Casey Turner sat at the diner's counter, which had seen better days and more customers. Her head was buried in her phone, searching various sites for a different job and a better life than the shitshow it had become. The diner was mostly empty, save for a couple of regulars nursing their coffees and the other worn-out waitress who barely glanced at her customers as she refilled their cups with stale, lukewarm brew.

It hadn't always been like this. Casey's life had once been full of promise. She'd been a bright student with dreams of attending college and becoming a fashion designer, but her family's financial troubles had worsened. Her father, once a hardworking clerk, had lost his job when the local hardware store closed. Unable to find steady work, he became depressed and turned to the bottle. Then her mother up and left. The house that was once filled with the sound of happiness became a place of silence and the odor of stale beer.

It hadn't taken long for discarded bills to cover every table in the house, and those with the word *DELINQUENT* stamped in bold letters stood out the most. Consequently, Casey had been forced to drop out of high school during her senior year to accept a string of low-paying jobs that barely covered the rent. She'd bounced from one dead-end job to another—dishwasher, cashier, gas station attendant—each more soul-crushing than the last. Her paychecks had mostly gone toward her father's alcohol rather than the rent. The stress had been relentless.

Still on her break at the diner, Casey continued to swipe her phone's screen, hoping for anything that might be the opportunity she hoped for. The ads were filled with the usual crap about part-time cashiers, warehouse workers, and nebulous entry-level jobs with no experience necessary. She'd fallen for those one too many times, and she needed something more, something that could pull her out of the quicksand her life had become. She wanted to escape from Oklahoma City, to find a place where she didn't have to worry about the next bill or her father's drunken rants.

Then, an ad caught her eye. It differed from the usual job listings because it was sleek and polished and promised something more.

> *Want to earn big? Tired of the same old routine? Travel, work in exclusive venues, and make more money than you ever dreamed possible. No experience required.*

Casey's despair had deadened all her warning bells, and while it sounded too good to be true, her desperation overrode her judgment. She clicked on the link, which led her to a flashy website with images of smiling young women in glamorous locations—beaches, nightclubs, and fancy hotels. A voice in her head told her to be cautious, but the promise of escape was too appealing.

She filled out the contact form by listing her basic information and availability. Within minutes, she received a response—a direct message from an account with a professional-looking profile picture of a woman in business attire. The message was polite and enthusiastic, immediately making Casey feel seen in a way she hadn't felt in a long time.

She read the reply several times and felt she shouldn't believe it—but she did anyway.

Hi Casey! Thanks for reaching out. We love your profile and think you'll fit our team perfectly. We can offer flexible hours, excellent pay, and even travel opportunities. Let's set up a call to discuss more. 😊

Later that night, Casey's phone rang as she lay on her sagging mattress. She sat up and nervously accepted the call. On the other end, a smooth, reassuring voice greeted her—a woman who introduced herself as Rebecca, the recruiter for the position. Rebecca spoke confidently, painting a picture of a life full of luxury, travel, and financial independence. She talked about exclusive clubs and high-paying gigs, meeting important people, and having the kind of freedom that Casey had only dreamed of.

Rebecca also promised to arrange everything: travel, accommodations, and paperwork. "All you need to do is say yes," she purred. "You'll be on your way to a new life before you know it."

Casey's heart raced. This was the chance she'd been waiting for, a lifeline thrown to her when she felt like she was drowning. She wanted to believe Rebecca's promises. She wanted to escape the suffocating grip of Oklahoma City and her father's crumbling life. She wanted to feel like she was worth something and had a future that didn't involve greasy diners and dead-end jobs.

"Yes," Casey said, her voice barely a whisper but filled with conviction. "I'm in."

The next steps happened quickly. Rebecca sent her an email with travel details and a bus ticket to a nearby town, where she would meet someone from the company who would make further arrangements for her. Casey packed some clothes, a few personal items, and a fading photograph of her parents from happier times into a backpack she had once used for school.

The following morning, she left Oklahoma City for good. As she watched the familiar streets disappear behind her, Casey felt a mix of anxiety and excitement. She was finally moving forward, finally taking a chance on something different.

Little did she know that the promise of a brighter future was nothing more than a carefully constructed lie and that the life she was about to step into was far darker than what she was leaving behind. Unbeknownst to her, the bus was taking her straight into the hands of the Chinese They were just cogs in the machine, moving pieces in the great puzzle of the Chinese syndicate's distribution network's sex trafficking operation—a world where dreams were shattered, and freedom would only be a memory.

Chapter 57 – Double Cross

FRANKIE PORTER BOUNCED DOWN the well-traveled dirt road of the Chinese grow operation in his city-issued vehicle on his way to an unannounced code enforcement inspection. His insides were doing flip-flops, and not from the rough road. He quickly wiped the sweat from his brow even though it wasn't hot.

Mei Zhao and Zhi Hao stood out front when he pulled up to the Victorian home. Seeing Zhi there didn't help matters any. Frankie had met him only once but had heard he was the enforcer for the grow. Somehow, they must have gotten word he was coming out, which put Frankie on edge because he knew what was at stake. The Gangsters Motorcycle Club had paid him $50,000 with clear orders: Shut the Chinese grow operation down by any means necessary. Frankie didn't consider himself greedy, but he wasn't stupid—you don't turn your back on that kind of money, especially when there could be a $50,000 bonus for shutting the operation down for a month.

When he got out of his truck, trying his hardest to look composed, Mei greeted him politely while Zhi had the look of a cold-blooded killer. Frankie purposely didn't shake hands with either of them because his hands were sweaty.

Get it together, he thought, you run the show here.

Mei said, "Inspector Porter, what brings you here today?"

Frankie forced a smile and tried to keep his tone light. "Routine inspection, Mei. You know the drill."

"I understand, but you always let us know so we can be prepared for your visit."

"Yeah, sorry about that. My boss set a new policy of no announced visits.

"Really?" said Mei, as her enforcer just glared.

Frankie began to sweat even more. He swiped a bead away before it ran into his eyes. Mei said nothing but turned and led the way to the first legal grow house. Zhi followed them closely.

Inside the main greenhouse, Frankie spotted a group of workers handling fertilizers without proper gloves. It wasn't a significant violation, but it was a start. He made notes on his clipboard. He also noticed a pile of discarded pesticide containers that weren't disposed of according to environmental safety guidelines. He scribbled on his inspection forms. After finishing, he carefully laid his clipboard upside down so they couldn't read it and took photos. He knew every trick in the book to get somebody when the situation warranted—and today was one of those days.

Zhi followed him silently, looking more and more pissed off. It made Frankie feel like a mouse that was about to be devoured by a hawk. Fighting to keep his composure, Frankie knew he was walking a fine line. If he pushed too hard, the consequences could be devastating—not just for the Chinese syndicate but also for the Gangsters MC.

Frankie completed his inspection. "Looks like you've got some serious compliance issues here. Improper handling of chemicals, safety equipment violations, and those containers over there"—he pointed to a corner —"are an environmental incident waiting to happen."

At that, Zhi moved around Mei to stand only inches from Frankie's sweaty face. In accented English, Zhi said, "You think these small things will shut us down, Inspector? If so, you play dangerous game."

Frankie somehow held his ground, though his heart was pounding so hard that he thought for sure they would see his wet shirt pulsating. "I'm just doing my job." His voice wavered slightly as he lied. "If these issues aren't resolved immediately, I'll have no choice but to recommend a suspension of operations." There, he'd said it, but he felt like his next move should be to run.

Zhi stared at him, not moving an inch. To Frankie, it seemed like a silent promise of repercussions.

Frankie finished inspecting the other buildings, then returned to his truck, where he felt the full weight of Mei's bribe money in his pocket—a burden heavier than he'd anticipated. The Gangsters MC expected results, and if he failed them, it wouldn't just be his job on the line. As he drove away, Frankie knew he had lit a fuse. How he would snuff it out, he had no idea. But he sure as hell was becoming a rich man.

Chapter 58 – Trapped

ARRIVING AT FAIRVIEW IN the evening, Casey was approached by a guy named Ben Thomas. He didn't say much, but said he was to take her to see Rebecca at the house where she would be staying. When she saw the van, warning bells began going off in her head. Nothing about it looked like the luxury of the dream job she had been told she would have.

As the van rumbled along, Casey's hands trembled as she clutched the tattered backpack full of her life's belongings. The van pulled into a driveway. Thomas got out, opened her door, and gestured for her to step out.

Casey hesitated, glancing at the house. It looked ordinary, with a welcoming front porch light, but something felt off.

Thomas yelled, "Get out of the van now!" When she didn't immediately move, he grabbed her arm and yanked her out, forcing her to stumble toward the house.

Yong Chen had been expecting the young American and opened the front door, his expression unreadable. He took in her disheveled appearance and the fear in her eyes as she hesitantly approached. He motioned for her to come inside, speaking in a calm, almost soothing voice that belied the cold calculation behind his actions. "Come on." He opened the door wider. "You be safe here."

Casey slowly stepped inside. A cold chill came over her as soon as the door clicked shut behind her. The atmosphere had changed. She was no longer on the outside looking in, and she realized she was trapped.

Yong led her down a hallway, past a tastefully furnished living room, and toward a door. Casey glanced around, noting the eerie silence and sterile cleanliness. It didn't feel like a home; it was more like a stage set designed to look like home-sweet-home but lacking warmth or comfort.

When Yong opened the door, Casey's heart sank when she saw steps leading downward. Sensing danger, she tried to pull back, but Yong pushed her forward. She moved tentatively, each step bringing her closer to the unseen danger she was feeling. The descent felt like a plunge into hell. When she took the last step, she could hear muffled voices of women speaking a language she didn't recognize.

Yong led her to the first room, off a hallway of doors with electronic keypads. Inside the small, windowless room was a twin bed with a thin blanket, a narrow table with a mirror and bottle of water, and a wooden chair. Casey's eyes widened in horror, but Yong's expression remained unchanged as if he had done this every day. "You stay here tonight, then upstairs," he said flatly. Get rest. We talk in the morning."

Casey was left alone in the cold, silent room. She dropped her backpack on the floor and sank onto the bed, tears welling in her eyes as the reality of her situation hit her. There was no way out of this nightmare. The walls felt like they were closing in to suffocate her with the weight of her fear.

Upstairs, Yong checked the lock on the front door, then returned to his routine, confident that Casey wouldn't be a problem. She was just another girl, another commodity in the endless cycle of exploitation that the house represented.

Chapter 59 – Turncoat

Frankie Porter sat in his new Ford F-150 truck outside the Fairview Police Department, his hands trembling as he gripped the steering wheel. Sweat gathered on his forehead, and he wiped it away with his shaking hand. He'd spent the last week dodging calls from the Gangsters Motorcycle Club and the Chinese, both demanding more favors. Playing both sides had seemed like a good idea at the time—a way to make easy money and keep himself on top. But now it was all coming apart.

He took a deep breath and convinced himself he was making the right move. The Gangsters were getting reckless, and the Chinese were becoming increasingly suspicious and demanding. He needed a way out, a way to tip the scales back in his favor, and there was only one person he could think of who might take the bait: Chief Jake Dalton.

Frankie walked into the police station, doing his best to look as official as the city inspector he was. Mary looked up from her desk. "Hi, Frankie. What brings you in today?" She smiled before adding, "Are you going to check us out for violations?"

"Hi, Mary, and no, of course not. I need to speak to Chief Dalton. It's about—well, it's important."

Mary knew something was up because Frankie didn't look like himself. He was sweating on a cool morning. But she knew Jake would figure it out. She knocked on the open office door. "Chief, I have the city inspector here to see you."

"Sure, Mary, please send him in."

Frankie felt his heart pounding as he walked into the office and saw Jake hunched over his desk, papers scattered everywhere. The chief looked up, curious.

"Frankie Porter. This is unexpected." Jake leaned back in his chair and didn't offer his hand. "What brings you here?"

"Thanks for seeing me, Chief. I've got some information." Frankie's voice sounded somewhat uneven. "The Gangsters Motorcycle Club has been running an illegal grow operation near the old Hanson farm. It's big, Jake. Bigger than anything else in this town. I thought I should report this to you right away."

Jake was immediately suspicious. A city inspector with this type of information didn't seem to check all the boxes. "And why are you telling me this? From what I understand, a city inspector is usually the last to know about these things."

Frankie forced a weak laugh. "Look, I've done some things I'm not proud of, but I'm trying to clean them up. The

Gangsters MC is out of control. They're expanding, taking more risks, and it's only a matter of time before someone gets hurt—or worse. I'm telling you because it's the right thing to do."

Jake leaned forward and studied Frankie's face for a long moment. The silence between them made the inspector even more nervous.

Finally, Jake said, "Come on, you're not just doing this out of the goodness of your heart. What's in it for you?"

Frankie swallowed hard. The moment of truth had arrived. "I'm trying to keep my job and stay out of trouble. If the Gangsters MC goes down, it makes my life easier. That's all there is to it."

Jake continued to study this man he thought he knew. He came on hard. "If what you say checks out, it could be the break I've been looking for. But make no mistake, if I find out you're playing me, there won't be a rock in Fairview you can hide under."

"I hear you, but really, this helps me because of some bullshit I got myself in, and this helps you to eliminate a large grow operation in our town." Jake had him write it all down for the record.

When Frankie finished, Jake took the statement, thus having probable cause to pursue it further. In the back of his mind, he knew he would need more firepower than he could bring to the table. He would work on that, but he had to admit, it was a good lead.

As Frankie left the chief's office, he couldn't help but feel a sliver of hope. With the Gangsters MC on the chief's radar, he could slide back into Mei's good graces, keep the money flowing, and finally have some breathing room. Perhaps he could even come up with a story to tell Mei how he provided the tip that took the Gangsters MC down. It was a gamble, sure, but it was his best shot at staying afloat and above ground.

CASEY HAD A MORE uncaring outlook on life as days turned into weeks of pure suffering. She'd once thought that she had it bad with her drunken father, but oh, how she would jump at the chance to get back to him and that life.

Forced into submission by her Chinese captors, it had been an endless stream of disgusting men entering her small, dingy room to perform acts on her that she couldn't blot out. Each day had been a horror show. Freedom had no meaning to her because there was no chance of escaping or getting the word out to anyone who might help.

She'd been on a strict schedule and forced to be available day and night. She had no privacy and no dignity. The necessities of food, water, and bathroom use had been rationed. She'd become just a body to perform sex acts with strangers, some of whom were violent and unpredictable or emotionally manipulative. She'd learned quickly to cope by mentally and emotionally withdrawing. Tonight, she was curled up in bed and hugging her knees. Tears flowed freely as she silently prayed for an end—any end.

After an uneventful drive to the Oklahoma Bureau of Narcotics in Oklahoma City, Jake looked around a large, purpose-built room with large wall-mounted monitors, videoconferencing equipment, and an interactive digital whiteboard. Special Agent in Charge Owen Wister sat among a score of other law enforcement personnel. SAC Wister's and Jake's first meeting hadn't gone well, and it quickly replayed in Jake's mind.

First, Wister had refused to come to Fairview to meet with Jake about his plan to raid the Gangsters Motorcycle Club and arrest the leading players. Jake had to drive an hour and a half to Oklahoma City, only to wait outside Wister's office for twenty minutes past their meeting time. Once in the SAC's office, Jake noted how Wister was seated behind a large desk littered with pictures of himself with a potpourri of Oklahoma VIPs. The man hadn't even offered a seat, so Jake took one. Instead of apologizing for keeping Jake waiting, Wister started with, "What brings a small-time chief from Fairview to a big city with big problems of its own?"

Jake hadn't heard that kind of posturing BS since he'd left the LAPD. But he'd decided to give the man the benefit of the doubt and cowboyed up.

"As I mentioned over the phone," Jake said, "I have corroborated evidence of a major illegal grow in Fairview run by the Gangsters Motorcycle Club. I'm here asking for your support and the resources to go after them."

Wister had squirmed in his oversized corporate-looking chair. "Listen, you're a chief of what...two other officers, and—"

"Four."

"Two, four,"—Wister waved a hand in the air—"whatever. I would be happy to help, but as we discussed, I need operational control of the entire task force. With all due respect, your four-officer leadership won't cut it. I lead one hundred and forty officers, and I have the experience for the operation you're requesting."

"And as I told you on the phone, that isn't going to happen. My city, my call. We can work together on this, but it's my play." Jake hadn't bothered saying that he'd come from a department with ten thousand officers and had probably directly supervised more men than Wister could have ever hoped to.

After some back-and-forth regarding overall command, both men had agreed to get the job done with Jake acting as the local coordinator and intelligence provider. Wister would have investigative and legal responsibilities, and the

Oklahoma Highway Patrol SWAT team leader would have tactical command during the raid. Even though the outcome of their meeting had given Jake what he'd wanted, it had still left a bitter taste in his mouth.

Jake returned to the present when Wister started talking to the personnel in the meeting room. Before turning it over to Jake, he welcomed members from his unit, the OHP SWAT team, and Fairview's county prosecutor.

After scanning the room to make sure everyone was ready, Jake said, "As most of you know, small cities like Fairview are getting caught up in both the legal and illegal marijuana-grow business. It's a billion-dollar industry that attracts players from around the world. Even in my community, we now have a Chinese-owned grow farm." A couple of people nodded their heads.

Seeing that he had their full attention, Jake moved on to the substance of the discussion. "My department has worked the Gangsters Motorcycle Club since I became chief. In the recent past, they were small-time criminals running firearms and doing modest drug dealing. When they got a sniff of the potential profits from marijuana-grow operations, they jumped in hard and fast."

Jake moved to the side of the room. "What changed the equation was our city's inspector. He confirmed what we suspected: a large illegal grow operation. I've run this by our county prosecutor, Mr. Roberts," Jake pointed out, "and he has green-lighted this operation. We have solid intel that the Gangsters MC is having a big meeting in five days at 1800 hours, and we will crash that party. If history's any indication, we should expect heavy resistance, so coordination between us is critical. Our objectives are to take them down, make arrests, and shut down their operation—without us getting hurt. Now, I'll turn it over to the SAC."

Wister slowly walked to the front as if he were going to accept an Academy Award. He had a remote in his hand, and while walking up, he flashed an overhead picture of the gang's headquarters onto a screen.

"What you see here is the old structure where they'll meet and where we'll make the raid. There's only one entrance." Using a laser pointer, he identified the only way in and out. "Our intel indicates they'll have at least one guard stationed outside, and they'll have comms to the inside. Further, we estimate that around twenty members will be at the clubhouse for the meeting and the party to follow. We've also confirmed the presence of a shitload of firearms and dope on-site." Hands started to go up. "Let's hold off on questions until after we hear from the OHP. Go ahead, Rich."

Rich Cunningham stood up, wearing his brown and tan uniform instead of tactical gear. "Thank you. We've worked this gang before, and they're tough SOBs who don't want to take the easy road. There was a shooting recently with three wounded—two of theirs and one of our own—and even though all survived, it's just proof that we need to take them seriously. So, our top priority is ensuring we all make it home in one piece. To do that, we follow a disciplined but flexible tactical plan."

Looking around the room, Cunningham confirmed there was no dissent, then used his laser pointer to highlight areas on the screen. "We'll have two teams. The primary team will be the assault team tasked with breaching the only entrance. They will handle the first point of contact with the gang members and will secure the main room by engaging any armed suspects."

He moved the pointer. "The secondary team will provide support and secure the area around the building to prevent any gang members from escaping through the windows. We'll have two snipers positioned to support the operation." He highlighted the locations. "They'll also provide real-time updates as they occur, especially before we form up to enter. We'll have one armored vehicle on standby near the location, and medical personnel will be available a safe distance away."

The second after Cunningham turned off his pointer, a rough-looking SWAT team member in the back said, "Chief Dalton, do we have intelligence on where gang members are likely to be positioned inside the building?"

"From what I understand," said Jake, "it's one room with a large table inside the door. Most of the gang members should be at that table."

The county prosecutor added, "I'll have no-knock search and arrest warrants ready for the clubhouse, so we're good to go there."

Jake said, "My officers and I, along with four deputy sheriffs, will establish a secure perimeter to keep the public out and suspects in."

"Okay," said Wister, "we'll stage a quarter mile away at the Oakley farm. Arrive at staggered times throughout the day and park your vehicles inside the barn. Assembly time is 1700 hours. I'll contact you with additional details as we get close to deploying."

After answering several questions, mainly about taking the building, Wister thanked those attending. The first big step to put the Gangsters MC out of business had begun.

Chapter 62 – The Plan

GEORGE SULLIVAN SAT WITH Li Cheng and his lieutenants around the large mahogany desk in the main office. The realtor-turned-crook thought of this collection of Chinese people as business leaders, but he wasn't sure if that was accurate. He asked himself if they were just a Chinese gang or part of a full-fledged syndicate, and he went with the syndicate because they were people he would never want to piss off. But no matter what descriptors he used, he had one for himself—rich.

Li got the late evening meeting going as the dollar signs whooshed in George's imagination. "I believe it's time we agree to do something about that asshole inspector, Frankie Porter. He has overstepped his authority. We've been paying him thousands, and then he showed up unexpectedly and wrote us up for a bunch of bullshit stuff. This has to end now."

"I agree that he's out of control," said Mei Zhao. "He's like a tiger mosquito that never stops biting until you swat it several times. It's time we swat Frankie, but I think only once should do it." Turning to their American frontman, she asked, "What do you think, George?"

George, who had never smoked until teaming up with these mafiosos, took a deep drag on his cigarette, then blew two perfect smoke rings. Everyone at the table couldn't help but stare at the perfect circles as they drifted over the table. "We gotta be careful. He's a connected, small-town prick, and I believe he'll go to the feds if we cut him off. But I agree that if we don't end our relationship with him, then he'll continue to think he owns us and will keep milking more and more cash from us."

Mei saw where he was going. "So we send a message."

"Exactly." George took another drag.

"What kind of message?" said Li.

As George exhaled, he held up his index finger. "Here in the US of A, we must be discreet and smart about sending messages. We can't gun him down because Dalton would be knocking on our doors within minutes. No, we ensure our man Frankie has a very unfortunate accident."

The killers sitting around the desk all squirmed a bit. In China, dealing with a problem like Frankie would have been simple—kill him, dump the body, and move on. Staging something added complexity that could lead to discovery.

Mei said, "His truck—that shithead drives drunk all the time, and the town knows it."

"Right on, Mei," said George. "Here's my plan. Frankie drives a new Ford F-150, which has the latest electronics. At night, he takes that curvy road past the old Hanson farm to shave off time getting home. It's totally possible that one night, as Frankie's driving home drunk, he sees he's going too fast for a curve, slams on the brakes, and—oh my gosh, the brakes fail." George took a puff and leaned forward to smash the cigarette in an ashtray on the desk. "He would die from an accident if he was going fast enough. So sad," George said with a big shit-eating grin. Everyone around the desk showed similar expressions.

NANCY DIDN'T SERVE JAKE his cup of early morning coffee at Rosie's, something she always did. Jake thought maybe she was off sick. As he was about to ask one of the servers about her, his cell phone rang. It was an unknown caller, and he debated answering. But given that robocalls usually didn't happen so early, he tapped the screen to receive the call. "Hello."

There was silence. As he was about to hang up, a familiar voice said, "Chief Dalton, it's Ben Thomas. Please don't hang up. I have something important to tell you."

Jake wondered why the dirtbag would call him after being fired from the force. "What do you want, Ben?"

"I know you don't like me—"

"Get to the point, Ben."

"Okay. I don't always make the right decisions—"

"To the point, Ben." Jake hated wasting time with the disgraced cop, but he felt he needed to hear him out.

"I have solid information about sex trafficking at a certain house here in town."

That got Jake's attention. Gossip had been swirling around Fairview about a whorehouse. "Tell me more."

"I dropped off this white girl at a house a while back. She was just a kid. Then I learned Green Horizon Cultivation was running a whorehouse with almost a dozen women, all Chinese except this girl." Jake kept quiet, wanting to hear more. "Look, I have to make a living, and my employers take care of me, even after my fuck-up exposing their sex trafficking at the grow. They weren't happy but liked my background, so they kept me around."

"Okay, so what are the specifics?"

"Before I give them to you, I just want to say that even though I do a lot of their dirty work, their abuse of women is something I can't handle. It turns my stomach."

Ben gave Jake all the particulars and then hung up. With the information from Frankie about the motorcycle club and now this info about a brothel, Jake felt things were finally coming around to put a dent in Fairview's illegal activity—and it was time to act.

Chapter 64 – The Assembly

As Jake looked around the staging area in the Oakley barn, he remembered what was involved in a raid of such scale. Everyone had finally arrived—the OBN's five officers, the Highway Patrol's SWAT team, four county sheriff's deputies, Jake's four officers, and two Fairview EMTs from the volunteer fire department.

All around him, the officers wore gear that Jake had worn many times when working on the LAPD's Fugitive Detail, including level III and IV ballistic plates and Gentex Corporation's Ops-Core FAST ballistic helmets to protect against rifle rounds. There was a good mix of firepower, including Heckler & Koch HK416 assault rifles and MP5 submachine guns, Benelli M4 tactical shotguns, Remington Model 700 long-range rifles, plus 9mm and .40-caliber pistols. Jake felt right at home with this team.

OBN agent Lila Hayes flew a drone over the target for up-to-date intel. Wister and Cunningham stood next to Jake. They had about an hour before showtime.

"All right, listen up," said Wister, and everyone gathered around. "I know we prefer to have months to prepare for this type of raid, but shit went down fast for this one. First, we've confirmed that the Gangsters Motorcycle

Club has a major growth operation, and second, we know that Gangsters MC members are gathering for some meetings and partying. So we get to be party crashers. Chief Dalton, what's your latest?"

"Thank you, SAC," said Jake. "There will be fifteen to twenty members present for the 18:00 meeting. We know they'll have at least one guard outside. We aim to clear and secure the site, detain all suspects, and shut down the operation. These are hardcore gang members, and everyone will be packing. I'll turn it over to Lieutenant Cunningham for the tactical plan."

"Thanks, Chief. We'll all head to the site on foot with our ARV standing by, but we need to stay out of earshot of the guard. Team 1 will move forward to concealment. Snipers will take position, and the drone will help lure the guard so we can neutralize him. Next, the assault team will approach, deploy their flash-bangs, and make entry. Team 2 will take custody of the guard, provide backup, ensure no one escapes, and then enter and provide support. The rest of you all have your assignments. Expect armed resistance— these guys won't come quietly. Let's all stay safe and take these bad boys off the streets."

"Eyes 1 to Breach 1," said Agent Lila Hayes, "I have one lookout armed with a rifle standing ten feet in front of the target. I'll try to move him toward your 20."

Carefully, Hayes lowered the drone to eye level about a hundred feet from where the lookout stood. Keeping the drone in a hover, she flashed the drone's spotlight on the subject. On her screen, she watched his head turn toward the lights. He started moving.

"Breach 1, the subject is walking toward your position. You should have eyes on shortly. I'm out of here." With that, Hayes maneuvered the drone up to one thousand feet.

Using his optics, the sniper took over recon. "Sniper 1 to Breach 1, the subject is on you in three—two—one."

"Police! Drop your weapon," said a member of the breach team as he jumped out of his concealment and pointed his weapon at the Gangsters MC guard.

The suspect turned toward the voice, raising his weapon as he did so. Just then, a second breacher came from behind and, using the butt of his rifle, smacked the lookout on the back of the head. The man crumpled to the ground. The two breachers quickly cord-cuffed him and handed him over to one of the deputies. The two rejoined the three other breachers gathered around their team leader.

Lieutenant Cunningham scanned his men and saw calm eyes staring back at him from the openings in their balaclavas. He was reminded how proud he was to serve with them. "Okay, stay tight, calm, and breach on my go. We got this." Five heads nodded in agreement.

As Team 1 approached the clubhouse, Team 2 flanked the building. The two snipers used their scopes to sweep the area.

Cunningham and his second-in-command approached the entrance carefully, their movements rehearsed to perfection. With a nod, his teammate wrenched the door open, and Cunningham hurled a flash bang inside. The grenade detonated with a blinding flash and an earsplitting roar, the shockwave reverberating through the room.

The breach team moved in. Cunningham darted left, his partner sweeping right and clearing the way for the rest of the team to surge in behind them.

"Police! Hands up!" Cunningham shouted while signaling the rest of the team in. He saw movement from the corner of his eye, away from the main table where numerous gang members were seated. A biker was raising a shotgun, aiming in his direction. As Cunningham dove for the ground, the biker fired two shots.

The roar from the shotgun was deafening. Buckshot smashed into the wall behind Cunningham as he fired two rounds from his HK416 rifle. The man was blown backward.

Cunningham quickly spun toward the ten men at the large table. His partner yelled, "Police! Hands up."

The men reached for weapons on the table and their persons. Some of the bikers dove under the table. The man at the middle of the table raised his 9mm and fired multiple bullets at Cunningham's partner, who double-tapped the suspect an instant before being struck in the chest. His ballistic vest stopped the bullets from penetrating, but the force of the rounds knocked him back against the wall.

Both of the officer's bullets struck the man in the chest, throwing him backward. A third SWAT team member saw this and fired two more rounds as the suspect went down. The biker hit the ground, dead.

Several gang members were screaming, "Don't shoot!" from under the table. But a man at the end of the table sprayed his semiautomatic weapon toward where the officers had just been, missing all but one SWAT team member, who was shot in the upper right arm.

As the officer went down, he yelled, "I'm hit." His right hand had lost all feeling. He efficiently switched his .40 caliber handgun to his left hand and fired at his assailant, as did three other team members. The suspect was hit with multiple rounds, putting him down for good.

The room was getting smoky, and the smell of gunpowder filled everyone's nostrils. Another gang member sprayed rounds from his semiautomatic rifle all over the room, striking one of his own in the leg. As the only shooter left, he got the SWAT team's full attention. All six fired in his direction. The man was struck multiple times, reeling him backward until he slammed against the wall and slid lifeless to the floor.

Realizing his team controlled the room, Cunningham yelled, "Everyone slowly get up and put your hands behind your head—now." As they did so, he radioed, "Team 2, I want two inside. Have paramedics standing by outside. We have officers and suspects down."

As the Gangsters MC members were taken into custody, Cunningham scanned the room. Four bad guys were dead, one was wounded, and two officers had non-life-threatening wounds. Firearms and baggies of marijuana lay scattered, and pools of blood were everywhere.

He followed the last suspect outside, and paramedics were tending to the wounded as sheriff's deputies and Fairview PD officers loaded the arrested gang members into waiting patrol cars. The coroner had been called to handle the dead.

Jake looked at Cunningham, who gave him a tired look and a bloody thumbs-up. Jake knew that with one less grower and distributor in Fairview, he could devote all his attention to the Chinese operation. He also knew the Chinese would be much more sophisticated and better armed than the Gangsters.

AN IMPATIENT MAN, FRANKIE kept glancing at his watch as he downed his fifth—or was it the sixth—beer. Ty had said he would be there by 10:00 p.m., and it was now 11:00. Asshole, thought Frankie. Little did he know that the leader of the Gangsters Motorcycle Club was a dead man and wouldn't be making any more appointments—except, perhaps, with the devil.

Frankie wondered what Ty wanted, but deep down, he knew. The Gangsters MC was sick of paying him off to shut down the Chinese operation and getting nothing from it. Frankie told himself it wasn't his fault. He'd written up Green Horizon Cultivation, but the screwed-up city had done nothing about it. He could explain that to Ty, and he was sure he would understand. Wouldn't he?

Looking at his watch again, Frankie noticed it was getting harder to focus on the numbers. Fuck it, he thought, I'm out of here taking his unfinished beer with him.

Two Chinese men sat in their car in the Black Stallion's parking lot, surveilling Frankie's shiny new Ford F-150. It was 11:00 p.m., and the lot was nearly empty.

When no one was around, Zhi Hao said, "Okay, Mio, let's go."

Both men headed for the truck. Mio was carrying a GSM module no larger than a deck of cards. The plan was simple: plant the device under the truck's chassis. Thanks to Mio, the go-to person for anything electronic, the device was set to override the brake and accelerator inputs remotely.

While Zhi stood watch, Mio slid under the truck and attached the magnetic device, which had a self-destruct mechanism.

Interrupting their operation, two giggling girls emerged from the bar and walked toward them. Whispering, Zhi said, "We got company. Stay under the truck until I give you the all-clear."

The two feet sticking out from under the truck disappeared. Zhi went to the back of the truck and pretended to take a piss.

The girls glanced over at some guy taking a leak behind a truck, quickly got in their nearby car, and left.

"Okay, Mio, finish up and let's go."

Mio activated the device and joined Zhi in walking nonchalantly to their car. Once inside, Mio pulled out his cell phone and checked the connection with the device. It was perfect. Zhi drove them out of the parking lot to get into a better position to tail the truck. Mio couldn't help but smile. He loved the device he'd designed.

Not long after the two giggling girls left the bar, Frankie decided Ty wasn't going to show up. The dude hadn't even answered his phone—all his calls went straight to voicemail.

Walking to his truck, Frankie thought that perhaps he was getting too creative by working with both the Chinese and the bikers simultaneously. But shit, the money was good; his new truck was proof of it. He never could have afforded the F-150 on just his meager city salary. A man had to be creative to survive in this world.

Once inside his truck, he pushed the start button. The big V-8 fired up and sounded so cool with the upgraded exhaust system. He headed for his shortcut home.

Frankie was a big NASCAR fan and had always believed that, given the right car, he could keep up with those boys. Coming to his favorite part of the drive, where the road was made up of sweeping S-turns, he imagined himself on the track battling it out with his favorite drivers. With his hands at the three and nine positions on the steering wheel, his dulled senses told him he was at Darlington Raceway, "The Track Too Tough to Tame."

Yeah, watch this, Frankie told his imaginary competitors whose headlights were in his rearview mirror. He jammed the accelerator as he approached one of the sharpest curves. There was a steep drop-off on either side, which only added to his adrenaline-fueled mood. He kept the accelerator down, prepared to trail brake through the curve. When he tapped on the brakes to shave some speed, nothing happened. He slammed the pedal—nothing.

He was carrying too much speed as he entered the curve. He kept jamming on the brake pedal, but no luck. With his foot pushing hard on the brake, the truck suddenly accelerated.

"Fuck!"

The truck left the pavement doing over eighty-five. It clipped the first tree near its top, hit the second one midway down, and slammed into the final tree at its bottom, snapping it in two. The fuel tank exploded and started a massive fire, but Frankie felt nothing. He was already dead.

Two Chinese men drove slowly past the flaming truck and offered no assistance. They were too busy celebrating.

Chapter 67 – Wreck

A BUGLE CALL RINGTONE sliced through the morning stillness. Reveille was meant to wake people; as any veteran could attest, it worked.

Jake picked up his phone and noted that his screen showed 0350 hours.

Sam yelled, "What the heck, Jake? You gotta change that ringtone. Maybe 'Rock-a-bye Baby' might work."

She was right, he thought. He didn't sleep alone any longer. He tapped his phone's screen to accept the call. "Dalton."

"Chief Dalton," said the familiar voice of the night-shift dispatcher, "sorry to wake you, but there's been a fatal accident. Looks like it's Frankie Porter."

"Frankie? The city inspector?"

"Yes, sir. Someone driving by noticed a busted-up tree by the road and stopped to check. When they got out, they smelled smoke and looked around. They found Frankie's F-150 down the embankment. I just texted you the exact location, and it looks like he might've been drinking."

Yeah, that would make sense, thought Jake, because Frankie was a drinker.

The dispatcher continued, "Em is on scene and handling the preliminary. Paramedics found an open bottle near the cab. They're calling it a single-car accident for now."

"Thanks. Let everyone know I'm on my way."

About twenty minutes later, Jake drove around a bend and saw emergency lights burning through the night. He was met by Em, who gave him an on-the-scene brief. Jake noticed that she'd already concluded that Frankie had been drunk-driving again and had screwed up and killed himself. Jake made a mental note to talk to her later about having tunnel vision during an investigation and jumping to conclusions because they were easy to explain.

He went up the road and began to visualize what might have happened, keeping himself open to anything and everything he noticed. The first thing that stood out was the lack of skid marks on the pavement. It seemed to him that if you entered a curve too fast, you would brake hard and leave behind skid marks. Of course, Frankie could have fallen asleep behind the wheel and run off the roadway. But Jake couldn't correlate that scenario with how high up the first tree had snapped. A truck doing close to the speed limit would have hit the tree lower. So Frankie had to have been going at a high rate of speed to stay so high in the air that he impacted the first tree near its top.

All of that indicated brake failure on a brand-new truck, and the chances of that happening seemed minuscule. He also knew that Frankie had loved NASCAR and bragged how he was always searching for the "edge." In racing, the difference between losing it and finding the sweet spot was tenuous. Great drivers found it more often than others, but most never pushed the edge far enough to find it. Frankie had never fit the great driver mold.

Continuing his walk around the accident scene, Jake checked the F-150 for any indication of it being forced off the road by another vehicle. He couldn't determine anything in the darkness.

He said to Em, "Make sure after the coroner removes the body that the truck is towed to the secure evidence garage. I want you to request that OSBI traffic investigators look over the truck's electronics and see what they can find regarding his speed, braking, and that sort of thing."

"Will do, Chief. But I'm just saying that I think you're spinning your wheels. To me, it looks like Frankie truly had one too many."

Chapter 68 – Saviors

CASEY TURNER LOOKED IN the small round mirror at the bruises on her once-pretty seventeen-year-old face. The worst one was the large black ring around her right eye. Seeing it reminded her of the bastard who'd yelled that he didn't pay her to just lay there like a lump during his lovemaking. She hadn't replied because she never talked to the men, so the SOB had smacked her several times, yelling, "How do you like that, bitch? Do you enjoy that?" She'd screamed for security, but the damage had been done.

All the men, all the violations of her body—she didn't know how much longer she could last. She'd started to consider suicide as a way to escape. And as Casey had that thought, the next man entered her room.

As Jake planned for the takedown of the sex trafficking house, he considered several alternatives. Putting an undercover officer inside was one idea. However, he'd discovered that all new customers were required to make an appointment and be interviewed through a coded messaging system. Other customers got in using an invitation-only phone number. He didn't like this vetting process and how much those in charge controlled who entered the house. The remaining avenue to get in was the existing customer referral system. But Jake knew that wouldn't work either.

After considering all the options, he decided on a no-knock warrant, which he got after he gave the county judge all the intel he'd collected. Fairview had a mutual aid agreement with the sheriff's department, and the sheriff agreed to supply two deputies for a planned raid at 0500 hours the next day.

At precisely 5:00 a.m., with the warrant in his hand, Jake stationed the two sheriff's deputies in diagonal deployment at the back of the house with eyes on each side in the event someone jumped from the windows. Both had been given FPD radios for comms. Jake and his four officers would make the no-knock entry, with him and his most experienced officer, Bob Spectrum, leading the team.

Just before moving into position, Jake activated a borrowed handheld signal jammer to cut off the security cameras' feeds to the monitors inside the house. He wanted to ensure that the element of surprise was entirely on his side.

"Team 1 to Team 2," Jake said softly into his mic. "About to use the key to the city. Stand by."

"Team 2, roger," said a deputy. "In position."

"You ready, Bob?" Jake whispered.

Bob nodded his head.

Jake lifted a breaching ram between them. Bob grasped the other grip. They looked at each other. Jake nodded, and they reared back, the heavy metal tool aimed at the deadbolt lock. They slammed the ram into the door.

A loud sound of breaking wood echoed through the early morning stillness, setting off several neighborhood dogs. Wood splinters flew as the door slammed open, its upper hinge broken. Jake and Bob instantly dropped the tool.

Jake yelled, "Police! Come into the open with your hands above your head. Do it now."

The officers split up, flashing their weapon-mounted lights to scan the area for threats. Jake saw movement to his left. A large man came into sight, armed with a handgun. Both officers lit him up with their lights, ready to fire.

Jake shouted, "Police! Throw down your weapon and put your hands above your head."

Blinded by the two lights, the man hesitated. Each officer brought his fingers from alongside his weapon's frame to its trigger. Bob started to apply pressure to his.

The man threw his gun down to the floor and yelled something in Chinese, which neither officer was able to understand. The man proned-out on his own as if he'd assumed this position all his life.

The three other officers making up the Fairview PD came storming in. First was Em, who slammed her knee into the back of the prone suspect. "Don't move, asshole, or else," she yelled. He cried out in pain and rattled off some Chinese phrases that no one understood, but they could guess what the words meant.

"Em and Billy Ray," said Jake, "secure the suspect and clear this floor. Joey, keep us covered. We're going up to the second floor."

Jake and Bob took the steps two at a time, their weapons sweeping the area as they arrived on the second floor. Jake scanned the darkened floor, noticing that almost all the doors were locked from the outside. He spotted one that wasn't. He pointed it out to Bob, effectively saying they would clear that room first.

As they approached the closed door, Bob reached down to the doorknob and looked up to see if Jake was ready. Jake nodded. Bob turned the knob, and Jake body-slammed the door open.

As he entered, Jake spotted a lump on the bed. It wasn't moving. Then he realized it was a woman wearing a sleeping mask and earplugs. Both men stood over her and yelled, "Police! I want to see your hands."

The woman stirred, then took off her mask. When she did, she screamed so loud it sent a chill down both men's backs. She was pale, her eyes wide with terror.

"Please, don't hurt me—I didn't know!" She fumbled to pull herself up, trembling uncontrollably as her gaze bounced back and forth between the officers' guns, which were pointed right at her face.

Jake lowered his weapon slightly. "Ma'am, we're the police. Calm down. We're not here to hurt you, but we need to see your hands."

"They...they made me do it," she whispered, her voice barely audible.

"Slowly get out of bed, ma'am," said Bob.

She did. Bob swiftly secured her wrists with handcuffs, then guided her to sit on the edge of the bed. He quickly adjusted her open robe to cover her more fully, ensuring she felt a small measure of dignity. Both men heard *clear* and a moment later, another *clear* as the officers finished on the first floor.

Jake toggled his mic. "Team 2, come on in."

The two deputies entered and took control of the first suspect. Em yelled, "We're coming up, Chief."

As they did, Jake exited the bedroom and deployed his officers in the long hallway, with a line of sight on five locked doors. He had Bob stand in the doorway to watch suspect two and the hall.

"Bob, get the key from her," Jake said.

She nodded at the wall by the door. Bob saw a chain with a single key hanging from it. He grabbed the chain and threw it to Jake.

After catching the key, Jake pointed at Em, indicating she should cover him as he put it in the lock of the first door's security device. All was quiet. He heard Em breathing hard, but nothing came from inside the room. He nodded to Em and she nodded back. He turned the key and heard the door unlock.

Jake went in first. Standing in the far corner of the small room was a Chinese girl in her pajamas, holding her arms to her chest, her eyes saying everything. She was scared but seemed to understand the officers were there to help her. She slid to the floor, sobbing.

He knew what would be behind the other doors, so he left Em with the victim as he went to another room. The next three were a repeat of the first. He ushered the other girls into the room with Em. When Jake opened the last door, he saw a white girl crouching in the corner of the room. She screamed, but after a moment, she ran to him sobbing. Jake barely had time to lower his weapon before she was wrapping her arms around him. He held her for a moment, letting her get it all out.

"It's gonna be okay," Jake whispered to her. "You're safe now." He could feel her body start to relax as her sobbing ebbed.

After securing the upstairs, the officers cleared the basement, where they found two more girls locked up. As Jake assisted them, he managed to pull his cell phone out and punch one number. "All clear. Bring in the ambulances and the interpreter. We have seven victims, one female suspect, and one male suspect."

"Got it. Is everyone all right?"

"They will be now," said Jake.

JAKE HAD SHUT DOWN the Gangsters Motorcycle Club's grow operation, and the subsequent investigation after the brothel raid showed direct involvement by Green Horizon members. Jake's case against them was getting stronger, and their grow operation would be next. Mary buzzed his desk phone's intercom as he considered the best approach. "Chief, Nancy from Rosie's is here to see you."

"Thank you, Mary. Please send her in."

As Nancy entered, Jake couldn't believe her worn-out look. It was as if she had just lost her best friend.

"Hi, Nancy. Is everything okay?"

She started to weep. Jake went over, hugged her, and sat her in the chair by his desk.

"What is it Nancy?"

She grabbed a tissue from her purse and dabbed at her tears. This wasn't the girl Jake had grown up with and had gotten to know again.

"I don't know what to do. I'm so scared."

"What's wrong?"

"Last week, while I was closing up, Mei Zhao and a guy carrying a gun came into my store. She demanded that I sign over my restaurant or else they would harm Timmy."

That startled Jake. They were taking their grow operation to the next level by being willing to kill to get what they wanted.

"That's horrible. Are you sure they threatened to harm Timmy?"

"Yes, they showed me a picture of him walking to school. I couldn't believe it, but I had no choice but to sign over my restaurant to them," she said as she wept.

Jake thought about it. "From now on, you escort Timmy to and from school. All other times, keep him close to home until I can act on this. We can't take any chances. I'll put together a plan. I'll keep you informed on how it goes, but I can tell you right now that whatever I come up with won't go well for those Chinese bastards."

WITH HELP FROM A paid interpreter, Jake interviewed the Chinese girls from the brothel. Kevin Yang was a business major at Oklahoma State University and the son of an American Taiwanese couple who had recently moved to Fairview. He was shocked when he first came face-to-face with the victims of the criminal sex trafficking operation, but fortunately, Kevin was an adapter and concentrated on interpreting what was said.

He sat with Jake and the girls in a small room without windows. Kevin thought the chief was an expert interrogator because he blended empathy with patience but always remained persistent. They learned the backgrounds of the six young women, two of whom were found in the basement, which were so similar that it was as if the Chinese syndicate used a recruitment boilerplate.

The girls had been coaxed from their disadvantaged homes in China by the promise of a better life working in the US. In every instance, the syndicate had loaned them the money to get to America, then charged extraordinary interest rates and kept all their earnings as repayment.

Once in the US, their passports were taken—if they had them. The girls were constantly threatened with violence if they attempted to escape or didn't comply with their duties. Ms. Rebecca, who was the recruiter and the madam who ran the house, had said if they didn't do as they were told, the syndicate would kill their families. The captives said they felt hopeless without access to phones, money, or anyone they could trust. All six identified individuals from the Chinese grow operation as people who participated in the running and upkeep of the house, so Jake had what he needed to link Green Horizons Cultivation to sex trafficking.

Next in was Ms. Rebecca. When she entered the room, Kevin felt like the temperature dropped ten degrees. As she took her seat, she glowered at him and said, "Look, you good-for-nothing son of a bitch, you fuck up what I say, and I'll personally see to it that you and your half-breed family don't see the next sunrise. Understand?"

Kevin looked at Jake and repeated what she'd said in the exact words, using all the voice inflictions she had used. Jake stared back at her and said, "Ms. Rebecca, I brought an interpreter in case you would be more comfortable speaking in your native tongue, and this can go one of two ways. Either you cooperate with us, or I will just put you back in your cell and move on to the next person. Do you understand?" Jake flashed her a sarcastic smile. She glared at Kevin while he translated everything, but she didn't say a word.

"You told my officers that you run the house with no backing or involvement of anyone else. Really?" Jake said.

"You think I need a partner to run a place like that? I was in business long before you decided to play hero."

"Right," said Jake, so you're paying for the whole operation—the rent, the utilities, and the security to keep the girls locked up. That all comes out of your pocket, huh?"

The madam gave Jake a dirty look. "I handle my own business. And I don't need a lecture from a small-town cop who doesn't know when he's out of his league."

"Well, you're sitting in my interrogation room, and I heard what you said when we first apprehended you. I suggest you cooperate with me, and I'll return the favor when I write this all up." He paused to let Kevin finish, then let the silence linger for a few seconds. "Is it true the girls working for you are prisoners?"

"You don't know what you're talking about. They were hired honestly and fairly. They chose to work for me. Nobody forced them."

Jake shook his head in disbelief. "Hired? You've got girls with no papers who barely know where they are, and you expect me to believe they chose that? Either you're lying, or you've got someone else calling the shots. Maybe even threatening you. Which is it?"

"Think what you want," she said. "It's my place. I set the rules. You don't have shit for proof linking anyone else to this."

"That's where you're wrong, Ms. Rebecca. I have plenty of evidence that the folks running Green Horizons Cultivation are behind this. So, if I were you, I would start talking, or you'll be the only one taking the fall when the whole operation is exposed. We're talking charges not just for the brothel but for international sex trafficking, so it'll be federal prison. Do you think the people behind you care what happens to you? Trust me, when the dust settles, they won't lift a finger to help you."

She hesitated before saying, "You're full of shit. You don't have anything on me, let alone anyone else. And don't think you scare me. I've dealt with worse people than an overzealous cop from Podunk, Oklahoma."

Jake leaned in a little bit closer. "Maybe. But unlike you, I'm not bullshitting. I've got names, times, and records of transactions—all pointing to the people running the show. If you think protecting them will buy you loyalty, think again. They'll cut you loose the second you're more trouble than you're worth. And you know that. Last chance—you either cooperate or go down for everything. Your choice."

"Fuck you. I'm not saying shit. This conversation is over."

And it was. Jake turned her over to the sheriff's deputies, who were waiting outside to transport her back to the county jail. He had enough to put her away and another charge to add to the growing list against the Chinese grow farm's operators.

For the girls, Jake made arrangements with a victim advocacy center that was run by Chinese residents of Oklahoma City. He was assured that the girls could begin healing among people from their culture.

After meeting with an older, childless couple Mary knew who lived a few counties away, Casey decided to accept their kind offer and live with them while she figured out her next move in life. Jake decided he would help.

The two pulled up to Casey's new home and parked the car. As she stepped out, he followed. When she turned to say goodbye, she wrapped her arms around him tightly, her voice barely above a whisper.

"Thank you for saving my life."

Jake held her gaze, seeing the glimmer of hope in her eyes—strong and unwavering. It was a look he hadn't seen

in her before. With a small nod and a smile, he turned and
walked back to his car, leaving her to a fresh start.

"THANKS FOR COMING IN, George." Jake could tell right away that George Sullivan wasn't the least bit comfortable sitting in his office, just a few rooms away from a holding cell. But that was all part of Jake's plan.

"Of course, Chief, whatever you need."

"George, you're a man of action. How about we cut to the chase?"

George was already shifting around on the hardwood chair Jake had set in front of his desk. "And what chase would that be?"

Jake leaned in. "The Chinese mob you work for."

George scooted back in his seat as if the extra two inches of separation would help his predicament. "What? Come on, I'm a realtor, and I do business with lots of people. The Chinese from Green Horizons happen to be only some of my many clients. It's called making a living."

Jake pulled a thick file from a pile on his desk and threw it in front of George. "Don't bullshit me. This file documents your illegal activities with them. I know you've been helping with their property deals, but it goes much further, doesn't it? I have proof of you assisting them with money laundering through Rosie's and your made-up shell companies. Oh, and did I mention tax fraud, zoning violations, and aiding and abetting criminal enterprises?"

George glanced through the first few pages of the file and gently closed it. "Chief, this shit is thin. You would be laughed out of court on this made-up BS."

"Perhaps, George. But think of the court of public opinion when word gets out how the Chinese syndicate, with your help, forced Nancy to sell Rosie's because they said they would harm her son if she didn't sign the papers. This is a small town, and when word gets out about all this, you might as well pick up and move on because nobody in this county will have anything to do with you."

"Where are you going with this?"

Jake took a minute while George squirmed in his chair. Jake knew silence was a potent weapon. After a bit, he calmly said, "I want you to work for me."

George started to talk, but Jake held up his hand to stop him and said, "Look, I'm only after the leaders of this Chinese mob, not you. I can make sure things go smoothly for you by using the power of the pen. You're in a position to know what's happening inside the mob's operation. I need intel—names, schedules, and deals. You feed me that, and I'll make sure your name is seldom mentioned in any official report I submit."

George stared at Jake while his brain searched for how to proceed. The first thing that came up was how the Chinese would retaliate. "If I agree, they'll kill me. You think they'll let me walk away if they find out I'm helping you?"

Jake sensed he was making some inroads. "I can protect you, George. I've got resources. But more importantly, I can keep you out of prison. Keep working for them, and it's only a matter of time before they decide you're expendable. You know how these people operate—they'll cut ties, and you'll be the one left holding the bag."

George looked down at the floor and said, "What happens if I say no?"

"Then I start turning over every stone in your world. And trust me, you'll go to jail." Jake paused, then added, "But if you help me, you might just walk away clean."

The room was noticeably quiet while George stared at the floor as if the answer to his problems would be etched on the old wooden slats. He slowly raised his head. "Fine. I'll do it. But you better hold up your end of the deal."

"Give me what I need, and we'll both walk away from this in one piece." Jake extended his hand. "Welcome to the right side of the law, George."

As an LA cop, Jake had the support of a large department, an aggressive DA's office, detectives, and more. If you needed it, help was there. But as the chief of a small-town police force, he had squat. He knew he needed help to take down the Chinese grow operation, and he needed it now. They were the big and powerful syndicate and would take no prisoners.

He considered the FBI, DEA, and Homeland Security but didn't want to involve the feds. The town residents were suspicious of any agency larger than their city council or one that didn't have Fairview in its title.

However, that stance was weakened when word came out that the Oklahoma Bureau of Narcotics had helped Jake eliminate the Gangsters Motorcycle Club for good. So there was some trust, which was good because he needed help.

Consequently, he was again walking up to the building that housed OBN and their special agent in charge, that good ol' prick, Owen Wister. Jake didn't like the man who mocked small-town America and who was all about his importance. The way Jake looked at it, Wister had better shelf his power trip and adjust to the idea that the Chinese syndicate moving into Fairview wasn't just a local problem but the start of something much bigger. Various Chinese organizations had already moved into Maine and New Mexico, so he was counting on Wister's ego to motivate him to take on a mission that could move him up the chain of command.

Walking into Wister's reception area right on time, Jake was met by a stern-looking woman who pointed at an open door. He said thank you, entered, and saw the man himself, who had a not-you-again look on his face.

Wister didn't get up from behind his large desk. "Surprised to see you so soon, Dalton. I thought my agency did an excellent job removing that motorcycle gang from Fairview."

Jake thought that was interesting since the FPD, the sheriff's deputies, and the OHP SWAT team's raid had also helped get the job done. But he was used to "climbers" whose only mission in life was moving up.

"I'm swamped today," Wister said, "but I made the time since you drove so far. What do you have?"

Jake took the high road. "Thanks for your time, and thanks for your assistance last week. To put it bluntly, Fairview is being overrun. A Chinese syndicate controls a sprawling marijuana-grow operation—part legal but mostly illegal—and their criminal activities extend far beyond that.

They launder money, traffic both laborers and sex workers, and use extortion to tighten their grip on the town. They even threatened to kill the kid of one of our restaurant owners just to get her to sell her place to them. I've got evidence, but I need your help to get indictments."

"Smart thinking. This is way out of your league, especially for a small-town chief like yourself."

Jake stared at the man. Even though he knew Wister was a total prick, he still couldn't believe what he was hearing.

"With all due respect," Jake said as calmly as he could, "Fairview isn't Mayberry, and I'm not some Barney Fife. I've got informants, surveillance, and enough probable cause to start tearing them down. But I can't move fast enough without OBN's weight behind me. These people are dangerous, and I believe they were behind the death of our city inspector."

"You've got guts, Dalton, I'll give you that. But guts don't mean squat without results. I can get results, but I need documentation.

Jake reached into his bag and pulled out a thick file. He plopped it smack-dab in the center of Wister's desk. It contained drone photos, financial records, and a list of known associates—all meticulously organized and tabbed.

"This isn't just my problem," said Jake. "It's Oklahoma's. If we don't stop them now, they'll spread like wildfire. You've got the resources, and I've got the intel network, the townsfolk's support, and the knowledge of how this operation works. But they'll only go down if we use something called teamwork."

Wister gave Jake a dirty look but flipped through the file, at one point pulling it closer to get a better look. After several minutes, he closed it and said, "Well, I must say you have done a fine job documenting this. It's solid work. I'll put a team on it, but make no mistake—if you screw this up, it's your head on the chopping block, not mine."

"Not a problem. I'm used to that level of responsibility." Wister promised to go through channels to get a grand jury to hear the case and issue indictments against the Chinese grow leaders.

Finally, things were moving forward.

Chapter 73 – Trust

GEORGE SULLIVAN WAS A shrewd man. When faced with a difficult decision, he analyzed his options and made the appropriate decision. That worked fine when dealing with his culture, and he hoped the same process would work with his Chinese bosses. He'd decided to tell them what Jake was up to. Maybe he would gain a few points in return.

As he rolled up to the sprawling Victorian home, a burly, shaved-headed Chinese man stepped forward—his cold stare and hulking frame suggesting caution. George hadn't seen this guy before, and the sudden appearance of fresh muscle made him wonder if his Chinese associates had caught wind of trouble and decided to lock things down. George got out of his car, making sure to smile. The man didn't smile back. He pointed to the house's side door and said nothing, although he did grunt. George walked toward the towering Victorian home, his thousand-dollar cowboy boots crunching the gravel. He kept repeating to himself, you got this.

Once inside the house, he was met by a stern-faced Mei who didn't nod in greeting as usual. "Follow me, George."

He went with her into a massive back room. Eight sets of eyes stared at him as if the group had been talking about him. Li Cheng was seated at the head of a table with his second-in-command, Zhi Hao, to his right. To Li's left were Bin Wang and Jun Zhou. Two guards stood on either side of the room, looking nowhere in particular but aware of everything. George sensed this wouldn't be like their usual meetings.

"You've kept us waiting," Li said.

"Sorry. There's a lot going on, and I wanted to be careful that no one was following me."

"Caution is good," Mei said as she sat next to Zhi in the only unoccupied chair, "but you know how we feel about delays."

"Yeah," George muttered, his gaze flicking to Li, who remained motionless but watchful. "I came straight here after it happened. I figured you would want to know."

"After *what* happened?" Mei said, leaning forward slightly.

"Dalton approached me, tried to flip me, and said he would cut me a deal if I gave him intel on our operation."

"What kind of deal?" Zhi said.

George didn't like the way this was going and shuffled his feet. "He said I would walk free if I gave you guys up."

The dead silence in the room told George the mob didn't like how this was going either.

"And what did you say?" Mei said.

"I played along and said I would help him. I figured by doing that, we could feed him false info and gain some time to move against him. Look, I'm no snitch. I've been loyal to you since I put my name on the documents to buy this place."

Li spoke up, "Why were you there?" He didn't look just pissed, but big-time pissed.

"He called me, saying he had something to go over. He didn't say what, but I should be in his office at 10:00 a.m., giving me only a half hour to get there. What the hell was I supposed to do? So now I'm here to give you information right from the chief's mouth. That alone should prove my loyalty to you."

Mei scanned the room, making eye contact with everyone but George. "Jake Dalton is becoming a problem that—"

"A problem to deal with now," Li said. He continued talking to the others around the table in Chinese, and everyone took a turn saying something.

George felt a flicker of relief as the conversation seemed to focus on Dalton. But Mei turned back to him.

"You've put us in an interesting position, George. On the one hand, you've brought us valuable information. On the other, you've allowed yourself to become a liability."

"I'm not a liability," George said quickly. "I'm on your side. I'm here to help."

Mei tilted her head. "That remains to be seen."

Li looked at one of his enforcers standing to the side with his back to the wall. He had the body of a gymnast and wore an immaculate black suit. "Take him downstairs," Li said. "We need to test his loyalty."

George took a step back. "Downstairs? What the fuck? I'm on your side. This is bullshit."

Li just nodded his head at the enforcer. The man grabbed George by the arm, pulling him toward a door.

George didn't resist as they descended into the dimly lit space. A metal chair sat beneath a hanging bulb at the room's far end. Two more enforcers stood on either side of the chair. George began to shake.

JUST AS THE GRAND jury was about to hear the evidence about the Chinese grow operation, Jake heard back from the OSBI investigators about Frankie's truck. He'd had his fingers crossed about getting any proof because the fire had engulfed the truck, destroying everything. However, investigators had said that recovering data from the onboard computer, specifically the electronic data recorder, was possible. In their favor was the make and model of the vehicle because the EDR was installed in a well-protected area meant to survive collisions and fire.

Over the phone, Detective Drummond said, "The EDR was definitely damaged. But if you don't mind me saying, we're all excited about this one."

"Don't mind at all," said Jake. "Anything helps. Fire away—oops, sorry for the pun. You know what I mean."

"Sure do, Chief. We extracted several memory chips and two processors and have special tools to restore those components for closer examination. We used solvents and ultrasonic cleaners to clean them and prevent contamination of the circuitry."

Jake could tell how excited Drummond was. Even though he didn't care about the process, he didn't interrupt as Drummond continued.

"We placed the chips in a specialized chip reader to extract data. Using our Joint Test Action Group interfaces with our in-system programming, we accessed the damaged EDR system entirely. Even though some of the data was corrupted due to the heat, we could reconstruct the truck's last movements using forensic software made for just this scenario."

Jake said, "I like it."

"Yeah, for sure. Let me give you our final analysis. The throttle was fully engaged during the crash, even though the accelerator pedal had no corresponding input. This suggests an external device was overriding the driver's controls."

Jake was excited about what he was hearing. "Wow, really nice work, Detective."

"There's one more thing. The data showed that even though the victim pressed the brake pedal multiple times, the brake system didn't respond. There was a loss of communication between the brake control module and the hydraulic system, which is indicative of tampering. A portion of a magnetic mounting bracket was found near the electronic control unit, to which a device might have been attached. I'm confident this was no random accident but a result of foul play. A planted device overrode the ECU, causing the truck to accelerate while simultaneously overriding the brake system. The driver was left with no control of the truck."

Jake knew precisely who had planted the device. He had to make sure Drummond's findings reached the grand jury. It was compelling evidence that would shut down the Chinese operation and put those assholes behind bars.

Chapter 75 – Loyalty

GEORGE WAS FLOODED WITH thoughts as he was pushed onto the cold metal chair in the basement of the Victorian mansion. The bright bulb hanging just in front of his face made it difficult for him to make anything out. He knew he had to quit feeling sorry for himself but couldn't help panicking. Breathing hard and fast, he looked around the room, trying to see anything or anyone.

The adrenaline pumping through his body made him fidget in the chair. A strong hand clasped his shoulder, forcing him to still. Then the hand disappeared. He couldn't even see who it belonged to.

After what seemed like an eternity of silence, someone—no, two people—walked toward him slowly and deliberately. They stopped just inches from him, but he couldn't distinguish who they were because of the light. One of them bent down, and after a few seconds, George could tell even before she spoke that it was Mei because of her scent.

"You have presented us with a serious problem. You contacted the police chief and expect us to believe you're not his inside man or informant."

"No," said George. "That's bullshit. I work for you guys and nobody else. My allegiance will always be with you."

"Shut up," said Mei with a bit of a growl. "Say another word, and Zhi will kill you right here. He'll then cut you up and grind you into fertilizer. Can you picture that?"

"Come on, Mei, I didn't tell the chief anything. You have to believe me."

"You say you're loyal to us, so you'll get to prove it. Right now."

"What do you mean—"

"Shut up, and let me finish. Here's what you're going to do. Out in the barn, we have the other traitor, Thomas. Yes, that Thomas, the one who worries about our whores more than about doing his job. Jake and his asshole friends raided our brothel and shut it down. All because of Thomas and his big mouth."

George started to reply, but Zhi slammed his open hand against George's face. The sharp *crack* of the slap echoed through the basement. George hadn't even seen Zhi's hand coming.

"Thank you, Zhi," said Mei in Chinese. Then she told George in English, "The only way you might live to see another day is to prove your allegiance to us. In a few minutes, you'll go to the barn, find Thomas, and put a bullet through his head. You may now talk."

George struggled to find any words. A vision persisted in his head of him blowing someone's brains out. But he wasn't going to be doing it to just anyone. He would be shooting his buddy, Ben Thomas. That was the most horrifying thought that had ever flowed through his brain.

All George could say was, "You want me to..."

"Kill him," Mei repeated.

"I'm not a killer." George started to sob.

"If you're one of us," she said calmly, "you need to prove it. There's no turning back. You either do it, or we kill you. It's very simple."

George could only think of saying, "What if I mess up?"

Mei laughed softly as she stepped back into the darkness. "You won't."

Chapter 76 – The Barn

MEI, ZHI, AND TWO bodyguards escorted George to the large barn. Just outside the sliding wooden door, Mei handed George a 9mm pistol. As she did so, both guards drew their weapons and pointed them at George, causing him to quiver.

"You know what needs to be done," Mei said. "We'll be right here to monitor your progress. Just remember, if you don't kill him, we will. And George, you'll drop right beside him. Now go."

George looked at the gun and wondered what he would do. Shit, he thought, he was a realtor, not an assassin.

George walked into the barn, and not even ten feet away, Ben Thomas was tied up against one of the large post supporting it. He looked up.

"George, what the hell are you doing here? Shit, man, is that a gun you're carrying?"

"Sorry, Ben. They sent me. They said you told Jake about their whorehouse, and he shut it down. I like you, but I want to live."

George raised the gun, his right index finger on the trigger. The metal felt strange in his hand. He didn't carry or use guns. He used a pen. But George took aim at Thomas's head and shuffled closer so he wouldn't miss.

Thomas's eyes grew large. He slumped down the pole. "Come on, man, we're friends. You don't have to do this, man. Please!"

"But I do." George tried to steady his hand, which had begun to shake so badly that he had difficulty taking aim. As he looked down the barrel, he saw Ben's face, and the fearful expression was something George knew he would never forget. He started to add pressure to the trigger.

"No!" George yelled, and dropped the gun. "I can't do it." He dropped to his knees as if the weight of what he'd almost done had forced him to collapse.

Mei and her entourage stormed into the barn. Zhi walked up to Thomas, raised an arm, and fired point-blank at the man's forehead. Brain matter and skull fragments flew all over the barn.

Mei bent over George's now-prone body. "Look at me."

George's ears were ringing. He first looked at what a few seconds ago was Ben and was now just a body with a hole in his head. He slowly looked up at Mei.

"You hesitated," she said. "That hesitation tells me all I need to know."

George's breath came in short gasps. "I didn't—I mean—"

"Sit up."

He pulled himself up and hugged his knees while he sat on the dirt floor. Staring at Mei, he waited for Zhi to shoot him. He wished they would hurry and be done with it because it was all too much.

"George," said Mei, "I could tell you were really trying to shoot Thomas. That counts for something, so I'll give you one more chance to prove yourself to us. I'm just not sure yet what it will be. Can you be counted on?"

Sobbing, George shook his head yes.

"Say it."

"Yes, you can count on me. Please don't kill me."

"Good."

With that, she and the others left the barn. George sat with his dead friend. Tears streaming down his face, George whispered, "I'm so sorry, Ben, so sorry."

Chapter 77 – The Shooting

JAKE WAS DELIGHTED TO hear that the grand jury had returned with an indictment against the Chinese grow operation. The indictment included drug manufacturing and distribution, money laundering, human trafficking, and even two environmental violations. Jake was planning to work with Wister and the OBN to serve arrest and search warrants, which would shut down the operation.

To help him celebrate, Sam joined Jake for a late dinner at Rosie's. It was near closing time, and the only other customers were an elderly couple. Nancy was nowhere to be seen. A woman Jake had never met before took their order.

Looking across the table at Jake, Sam realized she hadn't seen him that happy since their weekend in Oklahoma City. "Sweetheart," she said, "I'm so proud of you."

She kept talking, but Jake wasn't listening; he was eyeing the front door. He saw two Chinese men enter, their eyes immediately taking in the restaurant and settling on Jake. The two men were dressed casually but had shirts covering their waistbands. One of them wore a baseball cap pulled low. The other man was stocky like a weightlifter.

Sitting with his back to the wall at his favorite corner table, Jake's stomach knotted. He shifted slightly, his right hand sliding toward his hip where his Kimber Custom II sidearm rested.

The two Chinese men exchanged a glance. Baseball Cap nodded toward the table where Jake and Sam were sitting.

Sam said, "Jake?"

Both men reached for their waistbands and pulled out weapons.

Jake shouted, "Get down!"

Sam hesitated as Jake flipped the heavy wooden table over and hit the deck. Plates, food, and silverware clattered to the floor, distracting the two men for a split second. Sam dropped to the floor behind the table just as bullets ripped through the air and smashed into the thick wood of the table. Sam screamed while Jake fired two quick shots at the assassins.

Baseball Cap dove behind a booth while Mr. Stocky sprayed the restaurant with a continuous hail of bullets. Wood splinters flew as more rounds struck the table. The elderly couple was screaming as they made their way behind the counter.

Jake crouched low behind the overturned table, shielding Sam with his body. His ears rang from the gunfire, but he kept his concentration. Risking a glance around the side of the table, he fired another shot. Mr. Stocky stumbled back while clutching his shoulder, cursing in Chinese. Baseball Cap returned fire, forcing Jake to duck back down.

"Stay here," he said to Sam, his eyes locking with hers for a moment. She nodded. Jake saw her trembling but knew he had to try and flank the killers.

Moving quickly, he scrambled to another booth for better cover. Once there, he popped up and fired two more rounds, one of which just missed shattering the restaurant's coffee machine. Baseball Cap yelled something.

More chatter happened between the hitmen, and then they fired. Jake snuck another peek and saw Baseball Cap advancing. Jumping up, Jake fired two more shots, hitting the man square in the chest and sending him crashing into a booth.

As Jake was looking for Mr. Stocky, he heard a sharp gasp behind him. He looked back, and what he saw turned his blood to ice. Sam was slumped against the wall, her hand pressed to her abdomen. Blood seeped between her fingers and stained her blouse.

"No!" Jake shouted, his voice raw.

The stocky man, seizing the moment, bolted for the door. Throwing it open, he ran out.

Jake rushed over to Sam and dropped to his knees. Her breathing was shallow, and she was pale. He pressed his hands over hers to try and stanch the bleeding. But the blood kept gushing. Sam's eyes fluttered.

"Stay with me, Sam," he said. "You're going to be okay. Just hang on." Her eyes rolled toward the top of her head as she lost consciousness.

Jake heard the distant wail of sirens. He looked up as the elderly woman came over with a folded-up towel to put under Sam's head.

Jake shook Sam gently. "Stay with me, Sam. You hear me? Stay with me."

His chest tightened as he kept trying to get her to respond. Two paramedics rushed in. "We got this," said one. Jake forced himself to step back to give them more room.

As the medics worked frantically over Sam, Jake stared at his hands, slick with her blood. Messing with him was one thing—but shooting her? That changed everything. I'm coming for you, you Chinese bastards.

Jake wrestled with a decision: rush to the hospital to be by Sam's side, or hunt down the people behind the shooting. Knowing he couldn't sit idle at the hospital while those bastards still walked free, he ran out of Rosie's. He knew Sam would understand—if she made it.

He sprinted to the police station. As he ran, a fierce wind whipped through the street. Thunder rumbled in the distance, and jagged bolts of lightning illuminated everything around him, matching the fury building inside him.

He grabbed the department's Remington Model 870 SPS Magnum, which had a 6+1 load capacity. He knew he would need that and much more as he grabbed extra ammo. He then threw on his body armor over his civilian clothes. As he was getting some extra magazines for his .45, Em came barreling into the station with Bob right behind her. She wore civilian clothes, but Bob was on duty and in uniform. After a loud crack of thunder, the lights flickered and went out.

"What the fuck happened at Rosie's, Chief?" said Em.

"Two Chinese hitmen came after me and missed, but shot Sam. I got one of them. The other fled with a shoulder wound. I'm going out there to get him and anyone who gets in my way. You guys stay here and hold down the fort."

"No way," both officers said at the same time.

Bob added, "You always said that we're a team and function better on a hot call when we handle it as one."

"That's true," Jake said, "but this could get us all killed. I can handle it without you."

"We're coming, no matter what you say," Em said.

Jake knew arguing would only waste precious time. "Okay, grab your gear and extra of everything. We'll go together and park out of sight, and hopefully, this storm will make it hard for them to spot us on their security cameras. We'll hit the house first."

"Now you're talking, Chief," Em said.

They loaded up in Bob's 4x4 pickup, and Jake drove to the Chinese grow farm. Rain pelted the windshield, making it hard to see even with the wipers at full speed. The storm was winning the battle with the wipers and visibility was down to just feet. When they reached the access road, streams of water were running down it like a river. Jake sped up to keep from getting bogged down in the mud. As they neared the Victorian, Jake parked the truck just out of sight.

Seconds after exiting the vehicle, Jake felt the hair on the back of his neck rise. The air buzzed with static—heavy, electrical noises crackling around them. A split second later, the world exploded with a deafening *crack*. A lightning bolt struck a tree just yards away, splitting it in half. The ground shuddered while his vision blurred, as if someone had fired a shotgun right next to him. The smell of scorched earth filled his lungs.

"Shit, that was close," said Jake. "Okay, we're doing this just like we discussed. We stick together to maximize firepower, and handle each situation as it arises. If some of the assholes go out the back, we'll hunt them down after we secure the house. Keep a good spread. Let's go."

Jake barely saw Em and Bob nod their heads in agreement.

They were soaked clear through after just a couple of steps as the rain pounded them. Jake was leading, armed with his shotgun, while Em and Bob had their service weapons out and ready. All were carrying backup weapons. The lighting illuminated them every few feet as they moved forward, but they could do nothing about that. They continued towards the house.

When they reached the side door to the large house, the light above the door flickered as another bolt of lightning struck nearby. Jake tried the door. It was unlocked. He slowly pushed it open. Inside, they found themselves in the kitchen—it was clear.

Loud voices speaking Chinese came from the hallway to their right. As Jake, Em, and Bob inched along the hallway, the floorboards creaked, which seemed deafening to them but were almost unnoticeable because of the storm's pounding.

Jake peeked through the office's partially open door. Everyone in the room was focused on a burly man with a shoulder wound. He sat in a chair in front of a large mahogany desk. Li Cheng sat on the other side, yelling while pointing a finger at the man. Jake recognized the wounded man as one of the hit men: Mr. Stocky. Mei Zhao stood beside the desk, with two armed men nearby.

Jake stood back, held up five fingers, and indicated they would go in. Tightening his grip on his shotgun, Jake took a deep breath and smashed the door the rest of the way open.

"Fairview Police Department! Put your hands where I can see them."

Li froze for a split second, then dove to the side, knocking over his chair. Mei bolted toward the far corner of the room while the two guards drew their guns.

Jake fired at the guard on the right just as the man squeezed off a wild round. Jake's blast hit him square in his chest. The man started to grab at the wound but was dead by the time he hit the floor.

Em and Bob opened fire, their guns deafening as the burly man who had been sitting in front of the desk jumped up and returned fire. Bullets ripped into the desk behind Mr. Stocky and the walls behind the officers. Em was hit in the upper left arm and went down. Her gun came out of her hand. "I'm hit she yelled."

Jake spun around and shot Mr. Stocky, blowing him backward toward Mei. He was out of the show.

Em crawled to her gun, took cover behind an overturned chair, and, using her right hand, fired in the direction of the desk where she thought she'd seen a foot sticking out.

Bob and the second guard were exchanging fire. Jake chambered another round and shot, hitting the guard.

Unarmed, Li had crawled under his desk. Mei had ended up behind a large antique wood filing cabinet. After pulling a small semiautomatic handgun from her ankle holster, she began firing wildly at Jake.

As Jake dove for cover, Bob fired at Mei, managing to hit her exposed arm. She fell, and her gun slid across the floor, stopping near where Li could reach it. He went for it.

As Li grabbed the gun and started to raise it, Jake let loose with another shotgun blast, striking Li in his exposed head. Little was left by which to recognize the man.

The room went eerily silent. Smoke drifted like thick fog. Moans soon filled the void, both Mei and Em groaning in pain.

Jake placed an officer-needs-help call over the universal police frequency that small towns use. Bob went over to Em while Jake stood over Mei, who briefly looked up with devilish eyes and then passed out. Jake turned her over to handcuff her. Her left arm, broken from the gunshot, just flopped onto her back.

Propped against a wall and with her weapon in her good hand, Em watched over Mei as Jake and Bob secured the house. Approaching sirens could be heard as the storm ran out of gas, leaving it eerily quiet.

An officer-needs-help call is the one broadcast that prompts a response from anyone who hears it, no matter where they are or what they are doing. One OHP officer and three county sheriff units in the area responded. The two other FPD officers got phone calls from dispatch, and they jumped in their personal cars and sped toward the scene. A detective from OBN, who was pulling into a motel for the night, heard the call and quickly turned his unmarked car around. With red lights flashing and siren blaring, he roared off toward the coordinates that dispatch had given out.

Even though the house was secure, Jake knew it wasn't over. The entire grow operation needed to be cleared for possible suspects. He stepped outside to direct the responding units. Still gripping his shotgun, he took a deep breath of fresh air, and his adrenaline subsided. His thoughts turned to Sam, and he silently prayed she would be okay. He then thanked the Almighty that he and his officers had made it through the shooting. When the sheriff's deputies pulled up, Jake met them and laid out the plan to secure the rest of the buildings.

Soon, the large open lot next to the house was full of flashing emergency lights. Yellow tape was already going up around the Victorian mansion when paramedics brought Em out for transport to the hospital. Jake signaled for them to stop as they were about to pass him.

Em winced, her bandage already stained with blood. "Guess I'm not as quick as I thought," she said through gritted teeth, trying to manage a weak smile.

Jake grabbed her good hand and squeezed it as an ambulance pulled up. "Don't even start with that, Em. You were solid in there. You took a hit, but you kept moving and kept fighting. That's what counts."

Em blinked, her breathing shaky. "I didn't freeze, did I?"

Jake shook his head, a proud smile breaking through his serious expression. "Not for a second. You handled yourself like a seasoned veteran."

As the EMTs began lifting her stretcher into the ambulance, Jake leaned closer and lowered his voice. "You're a critical part of this team, Em. I'm proud of you, and so are the others. Now get patched up so you can get back on duty. We need you."

Em's eyes glistened. "I'll be back soon, Chief. I promise."

After they finished loading her up, Jake pounded on the closed back door, letting the driver know it was safe to go. The ambulance pulled down the driveway and out of sight, its lights fading into the dark.

Jake asked the OBN detective to take command so he could head for the hospital. "No problem," came the reply, and Jake was gone.

JAKE ENTERED THE HOSPITAL'S front door like he was pursuing someone. But it wasn't a person, just his anxiety, and it was getting away.

As he approached the front desk, the nurse looked up and did a double take at the soaking-wet officer, who was wearing body armor and had a few blood splatters dripping down his face. He looked like someone you would never want to cross.

Before she could talk, Jake said, "Samantha Taylor was brought in from a shooting at Rosie's."

The nurse realized that this was Chief Jake Dalton. "She's still in surgery, Chief. Doctor Patel's handling it."

"How is she?" Jake demanded as he unconsciously clenched his fists at his sides.

The nurse hesitated. She wasn't supposed to give out information on any patient—but he wasn't just anybody, and indeed, the police had a right to know. "The doctors are doing everything they can. She's stable for now, but it's a delicate operation."

He slumped into a waiting-room chair. The adrenaline drained from his body, leaving him exhausted. Minutes felt like hours as he replayed the events at Rosie's. He questioned every decision, every move he'd made, and every shot he'd fired. He'd let Sam down—bigtime.

Jake was on the nod when he felt a hand on his shoulder. He jumped to his feet. That startled Dr. Patel, who jumped back.

"Sorry, Doc, I'm a little punchy right now. How is she?"

The doctor's expression softened. "She's stable. The bullet missed vital organs, but there was significant blood loss. We've repaired the damage, and she'll need time and rest to recover."

Jake exhaled, the extent of his relief indescribable. "Can I see her?"

Patel hesitated. "She's still unconscious, but you can sit with her for a while."

Jake followed the doctor down the hallway to the recovery room. Sam lay in the hospital bed, pale but alive, her chest rising and falling in a steady rhythm. Seeing her hooked up to so many machines made his chest tighten, but he forced himself to stay composed.

Several hours passed. Jake sat beside Sam, holding her hand gently, his eyes never leaving her face. He felt nothing but guilt as he watched her. Letting her take a bullet would haunt him for a long time.

As he disparaged himself, he noticed one of Sam's eyes twitching. He held her hand tighter. Slowly, her eyelids fluttered and then opened. Jake watched as she took in her surroundings and finally noticed him.

"Jake?" she murmured, her voice weak.

"I'm here, sweetheart," he said, squeezing her hand more. "You're going to be okay."

She blinked up at him, a faint smile forming. "Guess I'm tougher than I look."

Jake chuckled. "Don't ever scare me like that again."

Sam's smile faded. "Did you get them?"

"Yeah," Jake said. "It's all shut down. Mei, Yong Chen, and several subordinates were arrested. Everyone else is dead, including the man who shot you. While you were out, I was told Zhi Hao and two others were killed during the clean-up operation. It's over, sweetheart."

"For now," she said, her voice barely above a whisper. "But it'll never really be over, will it?"

Jake sighed, carefully brushing a strand of hair from her face. "As long as I'm here, I'll make sure no harm ever comes to you again."

Epilogue

A WEEK LATER, FAIRVIEW began to return to normal. News of the shooting at the Chinese grow farm spread quickly, and Jake and his officers became something like folk heroes—especially Em. But for them, the victory was bittersweet. The scars—physical and emotional—would take time to heal.

George Sullivan was found hiding in his home; Mei Zhao, Yung Chen, and eleven others were arrested and charged with varying crimes such as conspiracy to commit crimes, racketeering, money laundering, bribery, several drug-related offenses, and human trafficking. The story made headlines across the nation, and brought attention to illegal Chinese-led grow in several other states.

Back home, Sam grew stronger with each passing day. She and Jake found solace in each other, navigating the aftermath as one. Their love, tested by adversity, only deepened. Jake's resolve to protect those he cared about had never been stronger.

One quiet evening, the two sat on the porch, a blanket draped over Sam's shoulders as they watched the sunset. Jake took a sip of beer as Sam asked, "You ever think about leaving this place?"

Watching the sky quickly turning different shades of red, Jake contemplated the question. He had sometimes wondered if small-town life was really for him. He missed the big city and the LAPD. He had so many positive memories, mainly of the officers he had worked with.

"I do think of LA and the department from time to time," he said. "How about you? Do you miss your work at the museum?"

"Nice trick, throwing it right back at me. I must admit I miss the city, the culture, and everything that is LA. But I also love Fairview and an unhurried life. But I'm with you. Wherever you take me, I'll adjust. I love you—I just have to get out of the habit of having you always save my life." She reached over and squeezed his hand.

Jake squeezed her hand back, thinking of the town he'd fought to protect. Fairview wasn't perfect, but it was home. Sam was right—life was good as long as they had each other, no matter where they watched the sunset.

About the Author

James Bultema is a military combat veteran and a retired LAPD officer with over twenty-five years of experience on the streets of Los Angeles. His debut novel, *Sea of Red*, became a bestseller, earning six prestigious awards and recognition as one of the top military thrillers. *Red Lines* became a #1 Amazon Bestseller on its release. With a degree in history and a passion for thorough research, Bultema ensures his depictions of police work and modern warfare with cutting-edge weaponry are as accurate as they are compelling. His riveting stories, full of unforgettable characters, resonate long after turning the final page.

Stay tuned for the second installment in the series *Invaders of the Homeland*, where Jake faces new challenges, dangerous enemies, and high-stakes action that will push him to his limits. Don't miss the next thrilling chapter in his journey.